The Shroud

By Father X

First Light Press

This is a novel about the burial cloth of Christ—the Shroud of Turin. But it is more than a novel. This is the full history of the Holy Shroud, the final understanding of its mysteries, and the terror and tragedy that today it has unleashed upon the world.

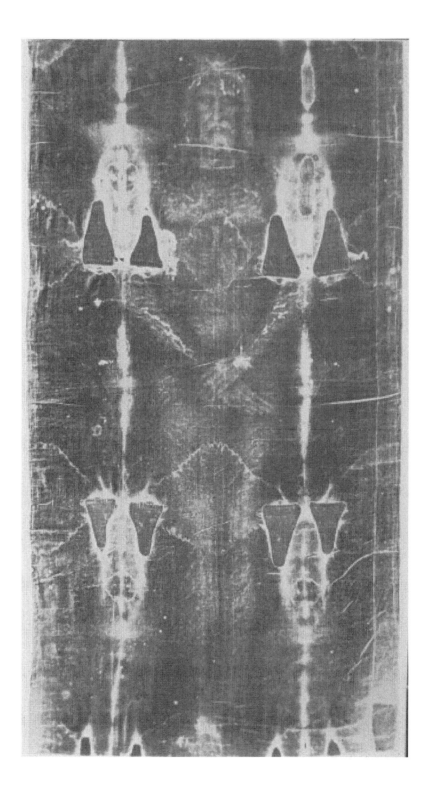

Contents

Foreword

History, Livy teaches us, is useful for life, so that we the living will honor noble men and, through our remembrance and praise, keep the glory of their deeds alive. Despite their sins, which no man is without, both Father Adrian and Father Balthasar deserve eternal life. May God have mercy on their souls.

But History exists for more than reflecting on great men and their actions. History allows us to hold the wicked in eternal contempt. Evil is ascendant in this world. How we have come to this juncture and why these confluent evils have so thoroughly overtaken Christendom, I share a glimpse of here.

In order to write this history and tragedy of Christ's Shroud, I have relied on a number of sources. The papers of Baldwin the Crusader, which the director of the Vatican Archives allowed me to read and copy many years ago, I have used to compile the opening chapters. The youthful diary that Father Balthasar wrote forms the basis of another few chapters. Finally, the detailed notes that Balthasar kept after being called to Rome, as well as the recollections of those near to him and to Father Adrian, plus all that I have witnessed on my own, tell the remainder of this tale—including the aftermath.

Forgive me—given all that has happened—for printing this book in secret and setting over it a false name for myself. Cherish whoever passes this volume on to you, since he is both your friend and God's.

RISE

Clermont, France

In the late autumn of the Year of Redemption, 1095, my older brother Godfrey and I traveled from Lorraine to Clermont. We left with a retinue of eight knights and three serving men to hear Pope Urban. With all the rain, it was a three-day ride on horseback.

The pope had called a church council there, one not only bishops and clerics but also we noblemen were allowed to attend. "This means," Godfrey said as we rode through sheets of cold, driving rain, "that there's more afoot than church business."

We had both heard rumors. It was said that Alexius, Emperor of Byzantium, was begging the pope for help in fighting the Muslim Turks. These Turks were threatening to conquer the great city of Constantinople. Godfrey thought the Universal Church might need our services. My motives were not quite as high. Whatever was about to happen, I was certain it would be an adventure.

The Council

The council lasted ten days. For most of the time it seemed to me an odd mix of this and that. First, Urban excommunicated King Philip of France because of the king's public adultery with Bertrade, his mistress. Actually, this was the second time Philip was excommunicated because of Bertrade.

"Perhaps the poor king just can't restrain himself," I said to Godfrey. People said that Bertha, the king's wife, was so fat she could hardly walk, so I really didn't blame Philip. Godfrey told me that I was a damned heathen for saying so, and would go to Hell. I knew the king's affairs didn't concern me, but I still thought I was right.

Then the pope said something that did concern me. On the eighth day of the council he declared that we noblemen must observe what he called "the Truce of God"—meaning that we Christians could only fight other Christians on Mondays, Tuesdays, and Wednesdays.

"This is really stupid," I whispered to Godfrey.

"Have more respect!" he hissed, and reminded me that I was going to Hell.

The only thing I liked about the Truce of God was that

Urban said that since the Turks are heathens we could fight and kill them every day of the week, even on Sunday.

During the last two days of the council the pope finally turned to really important business, to what we nobles and knights had been expecting.

"For forty years," Urban said, "the church in the East has severed itself from Holy Mother Church and from Rome. But now the East needs our help, so Alexius has come to us begging. He needs us to fight the infidel Turks."

Urban glossed over what it was that drove the two sides apart, but Godfrey knew all the details: "They can't agree on whether the bread of Communion should be leavened or unleavened. Each thinks the other side is wrong when it comes to the true nature of the Holy Ghost. And, of course, the big fight is over whether or not the pope should be the leader of the entire church."

None of this struck me as worth fighting about—it's not money, it's not land, and it's not people. So maybe Godfrey's right and I really am a heathen.

Then Godfrey added something that actually made sense. "Constantinople and the East are rich and civilized. Their churches and cities are golden and beautiful. To them, we in the West are more rough and tumble, more 'unrefined.' To the East, we are poorer, dirtier, and definitely more unruly. Besides, all the holiest places are there. Here all we have are ruins, woods, and goat farms."

"I'd rather fight the bastards who look down on us that way, even if they're Christians, than fight the Turks, who've never done anything to us that I know of," I said.

Godfrey, who had the bad habit of looking at everything

from all sides, snapped back. "Look around, brother! Look at this crowd of stinking peasants pushing against us. That's why the East thinks so little of us." Then he smiled. "And yet, it really is sweet that Alexius—pompous Alexius—has decided to come running to us vulgar and uncivilized ruffians for aid."

The following day, just before the council came to a close, Urban preached a great sermon before the whole crowd. It was the finest sermon I have ever heard. Urban spoke of how the Muslims and their religion had spread from the waste places of Arabia through all of the Middle East and across Africa, through Sicily, and into Spain. They had overrun Carthage, the home of Saint Augustine. They slaughtered Christians in the ancient patriarchies of Antioch and Alexandria. Worst of all, they had conquered Jerusalem and taken command of the most sacred shrine in all Christendom—the Church of the Holy Sepulcher—the church built over the tomb where Christ's body once rested, before His glorious resurrection.

But now, if we stood together to help the emperor defeat the heathens before they took Constantinople, not only would we be doing a wonderful thing for Our Lord, but the East would once again be indebted to Rome and the West. And maybe, just maybe, it might be the start of rolling back the invaders from Spain and Sicily, too.

In urging us to win back Jerusalem and free it from the heathens, the pope spoke about all that would be gained: the defeat of Islam, which had done so much evil in the world; the loyalty of Byzantium; the recapture of the ancient great patriarchies; and, God willing, the reunification of all Christendom under his papacy.

"And if we are successful," Pope Urban proclaimed, "there will be land for peasants, glory for knights, and the remission of all sins for those of you who die in the cause!" He ended by exhorting us that it is now within *our* power and has become *our* sacred duty to destroy this murderous people, this vile race of Muslims!

Even before Urban finished, I turned to Godfrey and whispered eagerly, "Do you see how wonderful this will be? We can return with a caravan of gold from Constantinople! And think of the adventure and the glory that will be ours! We'll slaughter so many heathens in liberating Jerusalem that our names will be heralded throughout France."

"You're worse than any heathen," my brother retorted. "We'll do this for our Sacred Lord, not for your greed or your pride. It's our holy obligation. We do this not for you, nor for me, nor even for the pope. We do this because God wills it."

As Urban finished speaking the now frenzied assembly picked up where Godfrey left off and began shouting. "*Deus lo volt! Deus lo volt!*"—"God wills it! *God* wills it!"

"With such passion," I cried to Godfrey over the chanting, "there's no way this cannot work."

The Three Brothers

After the council, Godfrey and I returned to Lorraine and teamed up with our older brother, Eustace. We had heard that Raymond of Toulouse was already raising an army to help protect Constantinople and liberate Jerusalem. Even though he had only one eye, Raymond was a decent enough fighter. But unlike our family, Raymond's title was new. In fact, he owed it to Urban, who for certain favors not only declared Raymond the rightful Count of Toulouse, but gave him title to all of Provence as well.

Money holds sway everywhere in this world.

Still, I was pretty sure that Godfrey, Eustace, and I together were richer than Raymond—and I knew that we could pull together just as fierce an army. Just as I was certain that the three of us and our men at arms would be the ones to protect the East, liberate Jerusalem, and save all of Christendom!

Jerusalem: 1099

B y the fall of 1096 my brothers and I had raised an army of twenty thousand fighting men from all parts of northern France. Leaving Lorraine, we followed the road to Cologne and Mainz down into Hungary. Heading further south and east, we reached the walls of Constantinople two days before Christmas, and offered our services to Emperor Alexius.

In the year it took us to gather our army and march it through Europe to the East, a pitiful mix of peasants and village rabble, with perhaps more women and children than able-bodied men, had already gone before us. They had no knights or noblemen leading them; no one, really, except a holy man named Peter whom everyone called "the Hermit."

Neither they nor the Hermit knew anything about war. They just marched, praying and chanting hymns as if singing were enough to beat back the infidel! When they reached Constantinople Alexius—who had no need for all these useless mouths to feed—sent them to fight across the Bosporus. Within a few days the Turks had slaughtered almost every one of these poor souls. Perfidious Alexius, by sending them unguarded he knew this would be the outcome!

But if any good came out of such butchery it was that I swore to myself that I would never trust the emperor. Nevertheless, and against my better judgment and protestations, Godfrey insisted we join forces with Alexius and his soldiers.

"They know the land," he argued, "and they're decent fighters. We can't win without them."

So my brothers and I put aside our qualms and marched with Alexius's forces. On June 19 in the year of grace 1097 we had our first victory over the Muslims. We captured the city of Nicaea. But without our knowledge, Alexius had already sent an emissary into Nicaea. In exchange for certain promises, the emperor had the city surrender only to his soldiers, not to us. He had told them that we were barbarians who, given the chance, would slaughter them all.

Having let the emperor's forces through the gates, the whole wealth of Nicea now belonged to Alexius, leaving us nothing.

Godfrey seemed willing to overlook the emperor's faithlessness regarding the lives of peasants and children when we first began fighting beside his men, but now he couldn't ignore the fact that that "the Emperor of the East" was little more than an ungrateful dog and filthy traitor. We vowed that Alexius could, from this day forward, defend Constantinople by himself.

Surrounded by our own knights and soldiers, we three brothers headed toward Jerusalem.

From Nicaea and Iconium through Caesarea we marched

toward Antioch. Beautiful, splendid, magnificent Antioch! For eight long months we fought outside its walls. Finally, Eustace and I figured out a way to bribe a tower guard. A full year after Nicaea fell, we finally entered the city. The riches of old Nicaea were as nothing compared to the splendors of Antioch.

Unfortunately, it was Antioch where we brothers had our first serious conflict. Eustace and I wanted to kill all the inhabitants and take what we could. Godfrey was against killing anyone, including soldiers.

"These people did nothing more than defend their city," Godfrey insisted. "They are not our enemies; we *made* them our enemies. We should take what we need to finish our journey to Jerusalem and leave Antioch's inhabitants in peace."

Eustace and I agreed that the townspeople fought nobly and in their own defense. Still, they did not surrender, but were defeated. And now their nobility and bravery would cost them. We overruled Godfrey's objections and supported by our men at arms, put to the sword virtually everyone, including the young.

But just as we visited necessary slaughter on the enemy, so we found ourselves imperiled. In the months after departing Antioch, a plague broke out. Godfrey blamed the pestilence on our sin in killing the Antiochans, and perhaps he was right. But there was nothing we could do about that now.

On top of the plague, the sands and winds of Syria were so fierce that what started as a force of over 5,000 glorious knights and 15,000 soldiers and bowmen had withered down to 1,500 knights and fewer than 4,000 soldiers. Our situation became so dire that every village we entered on our way to Jerusalem—even those, I admit, whose inhabitants willingly surrendered to us—we despoiled.

Still, despite every hardship Satan put in our path, we continued our march to Jerusalem.

And it was with this ragged remnant of knights and soldiers that on June 7, 1099, my brothers and I finally undertook what we desired with all our souls: the siege of Jerusalem.

And on July 15, three and a half years after Pope Urban first preached the crusade, we entered the city.

Whether it was hunger or thirst or simply the cruel joy of victory, before the sun set the next day our men had killed almost the entire population of God's Holy City. Jews, Muslims, Christians loyal to Alexius and the Eastern Church, women, children—we spared no one. And no one, not even Godfrey, could restrain our bloodthirsty men. So great was the slaughter that the sand beneath our feet couldn't hold it and the blood of its people pooled throughout Jerusalem.

Soon the mounds of rotting bodies caused a stench beyond endurance. The few infidels we kept alive as our slaves had as their first task dragging the dead through the gates of the city, to pile in immense heaps and burn. I could not believe that anyone before this time ever saw or heard of such slaughter. Funeral pyres as great as the pyramids were built from pagan bodies. And to this day no one knows their number except God alone.

Raymond of Toulouse, who was close to Urban and whose forces had joined with ours in storming the great city, was offered the kingship of Jerusalem. He declined.

"I will not wear a crown of gold where Christ once wore a crown of thorns."

Godfrey also declined the title, but allowed himself to be called *Advocatus Sancti Sepulchri*—"Protector of the Holy Sepulcher." This was sufficient.

But within a year Raymond had left to fight in Tripoli, where he was killed, and Godfrey was also dead. I succeeded him, and was persuaded that the title "King of Jerusalem" should rightly be mine.

And in all holy humility, after having a great Thanksgiving Mass said and the singing of the *Te Deum*, I became Baldwin, King of Jerusalem.

I have written this so that the entire world might know that ours was a venture of unparalleled hardships and infinite daring. Through us and the force of our arms, the Saracens lost their hold on Christ's Holy City—and from that day onward we knew the world would be always and forever changed.

Truly was it proclaimed, *"Deus lo volt!"*

Rome: 2009

On April 9, 2009, Sister Maria Fidelis, from the order of Augustinian nuns living within the Vatican, and Sister St. Rose of the Sisters of Charity were leaving the Church of Santissima Trinità dei Pellegrini in Rome. It was late evening. They were on their way back to their car, and then to their small convent in the Vatican.

Both had permission to travel to this service, since Sister St. Rose had been asked to sing in the choir for Holy Thursday liturgy. Almost as important, the convent had filled a basket of breads and cakes to leave in the door of the Office for Refugees on Via delle Zoccollette, "the street of the small clogs," just a few blocks away from the great church.

The two had stayed later than they should have, praying at the magnificently lit Altar of Repose long after the service had ended.

"Have you ever seen so many candles?" Sister St. Rose whispered to Sister Maria. "There must be a thousand!"

Sister Maria nodded and continued praying.

By the time they had left the church and were turning the corner to where their car was parked, a fairly strong rain pelted the empty streets.

"Have you ever noticed how it always seems to rain on Holy Thursday?" Sister St. Rose observed as they neared the car. "For as long as I can remember it has always rained. I have a cousin in New York City who says it always rains there, too. I don't know why, but it does seem to be true. Have you noticed?"

Sister Maria was about to respond when five dark youths leaped from the shadows and beat them, pocketing whatever small cash they could find on the battered women. Then the youngest of the gang grabbed Sister St. Rose in a chokehold. Holding his hand over her mouth, he watched the others hold Sister Maria down as the oldest one raped her.

It was over quickly. Staring in horror at Sister Maria lying in the mud beside their car, Sister St. Rose struggled wildly and bit the hand of the boy stifling her screams. He stumbled back with a yelp. Teeth bared, he pulled a small dagger from his waistband and leapt forward. He struck the nun, who was reaching for Sister Maria, across her upper arm. "*Let's go,*" the oldest thug hissed as Sister St. Rose slumped, landing beside Sister Maria, their blood mingling on the wet cobblestone.

Without a sound five narrow shadows disappeared into the darkness.

Thus what began in Old Jerusalem a thousand years before was now circling back to the New Jerusalem: Rome.

Darwin's Pigeons

I t was one of those clear blue fall Italian mornings in Calabria. Papa was working with a serviceman from New York, U.S. Army Major Anthony Rizzo. Papa kept trying to call him by his military title, but the major always replied, "Please, call me Tony."

Tony had left Italy few years ago, right after the war, but recently returned with his new bride, a beautiful, shy Irish American girl named Margaret. He called her "Meg."

You see, Papa and Uncle Domenico had opened our house and farm to America during the war, and the American soldiers, in turn, kept us safe—not only from Mussolini's soldiers but also from the many Fascist partisans in town. When the war was over, Papa told the departing Americans, "If you ever want return to live here, I have enough land, even some small houses, on the farm. Choose one, fix it up, and it's yours. It would be my honor, my way of repaying you for your service in liberating Italy—and for saving my family."

I was born by then, so I guess that meant they had saved me, too.

Tony was the only one who came for good, although

others visited us over the years. He and Meg picked out an old stone building with a red tile roof about half a kilometer from our house. Even though it had no electricity or heat and was missing a door and a few windows, Meg thought it was lovely. "It has water, Tony, and there's room for a big garden!"

Although I always thought Tony was funny looking—short, balding, bulbous nose—he deserved a beautiful wife because he was *good*. He was an army surgeon, and while stationed on our property, Tony did everything from saving wounded soldiers to treating Papa after he'd been shot in the leg to saving a cow and her calf during an unexpectedly difficult birth. I think Tony loved the animals on our farm as much as I did.

One day, he approached me with a deal: "Balthasar, if you'll help Meg learn Italian, I'll bring you some pigeons from New York on my next trip back."

He knew how much I loved pigeons. I took care of a few rag-tag birds in an old coop Papa built years ago on the roof of our farmhouse, but the pigeons Tony brought back from New York City were really special.

He brought me four different mated pairs. "This kind will fly straight up, then tumble over and over backwards before they straighten out a few feet above the coop and flutter down," Tony explained to me. Another pair was large and mottled with long necks and pearl eyes that Tony said were found only in New York. Now I had the only pair in all of Italy! Another pair were fantails, one blue and one white. These are beautiful birds. I'd only seen this kind once before, on a family trip to Naples. "Beautiful, yes," Tony said, "but not great fliers. And truth be known, they're actually pretty dumb. But they strut around like they own the place with their big tails up in the air. They'll make you happy."

But my favorite was a pair of the most exotic pigeons I'd ever seen. Small and friendly, they had dappled almond feathers, little peaks on the crown of their heads, and a ruffled neck, just as if they were wearing small bow ties.

Tony also brought me a book about Charles Darwin, the great scientist. "Darwin bred pigeons throughout his life," he said. "Long before he went on his famous voyages to the Galapagos Islands, he studied pigeons and pigeon genetics. This was when he first began to see that all of the varieties of life could have descended from a few, perhaps even one, original source."

Soon I would come to see for myself that it was through pigeons that Darwin proved that human ingenuity and effort could make perfect the characteristics of different species—even surpassing the efforts of Nature.

A few weeks later, when I was halfway through the book on Darwin, I released the birds early for a quick fly around the roof before I put out their feed. The day was crisp and cloudless. Then, from *absolutely nowhere* two hawks descended on the flock, scattering them everywhere. I'd never seen two hawks work a flock together—and they were deadly. One hawk lunged and carried off an older mixed-breed bird. The second shot straight down like a bullet toward my favorite bird. Just as he reached her, she turned and dove straight for the coop. She made it! But the hawk's talons ripped her crop wide open—right through where the ruffle of feathers had been.

I ran and grabbed a needle and thread from Mama's sewing basket. I'd never done this before, and I almost got sick pushing the needle through living flesh. *Almost.* I sewed the bird's front together again as best I could, and by the next day, she was eating and drinking.

Something so near death was now—*thanks to me*—alive.

The next time I saw Tony I showed him what I had done, beaming when he exclaimed, "Not bad at all! I guess you really saved her." Then he added, "I don't think I ever asked, but what do you want to be when you're older?"

I stared at the ground. "I never really thought about it. Just stay on the farm, I guess, and keep taking care of the animals."

I was shocked, then pleased when Tony shook his head. "I don't think so. I think you should be a doctor." Tony said he'd been watching me. "The way you took care of this pigeon, the way you care for all the animals on the farm—you can do the same with people."

When I think back to this conversation there are times I wonder if Tony was just trying to be nice to me, but I believed him. If Tony thought I could be a doctor, I was certain I could be a doctor as well.

Having It All

My name is Balthasar Castellani. I was born near the end of the Second World War to a large and once prosperous Calabrian farming family. Although the war destroyed most of our land and livestock, Papa always said that our family's great distress actually began almost a decade earlier. You see, we Castellani were always out of place: a well-off family living amid the harsh poverty of the countryside, with a decidedly outspoken and anti-Fascist father in an Italy caught up in the brutal nationalism and even more brutal anti-Semitism of the day. Our views gave the Fascist authorities in Rome all the reason they needed to expropriate the better part of our family's wealth. Later, as the war wore on, the neighboring rabble made any number of thieving forays onto our land and even into our home—further diminishing family resources.

Throughout it all, as Papa also always said, the Castellani spirit never broke. It was rumored, and I'm sure it was true, that we sometimes hid Jews in secret tunnels beneath the wine cellar and under the floor of the private chapel. And it was well-known that whenever an anti-Fascist tract appeared on the post office door or outside the parish cemetery that it was Francesco, my father, and his brothers, Domenico and Luciano, who posted it. Nevertheless, it took the march of the Allies from Sicily up the toe of Italy and into the southern countryside in the fall of 1943 to put a stop our struggles.

Little by little our family rebuilt the house and got the farm going again. Within a few years the family fortunes were more or less restored. In the early 1950s, Papa was voted mayor of our town—by the same neighborhood rabble who'd once caused him such grief.

I was Francesco and Elisabetta Castellani's first son, and I soon had two younger brothers. Even though I fancied that I was named "Balthasar" after one of the Wise Men who came from the East to visit Jesus at His birth, Mama said I was actually named for my great-grandfather, Baldassare. My great-grandfather, she told me, took up arms on the side of the Church against Garibaldi, though it seems that his only military distinction was managing to get himself killed in a minor skirmish near Salerno.

Looking back on that day when Tony suggested I become a doctor, I don't know why it took me by such surprise. On the farm, no lamb was born without my being there to assist, no goat was ever sick without my ministering to it. Back then I thought that if I were ever going to be something other than a farmer, I might be a priest, helping and pastoring people and not simply animals. But now, thanks to Tony's encouragement, I set my sights on having it all— and became a priest and a doctor as well.

Although I was hardly the first Castellani to join the

priesthood, I was certainly the first family member to attend an important university and become, as Papa would tell everyone within hearing, "a serious and learned physician." Again, this was blessed Major Anthony Rizzo's doing, or, actually, his wife's. You see, Meg's brother was an administrator at Georgetown, a Catholic university in America, and she and Tony convinced him that I had great promise. So, when it came time for me to go to college, I found myself in in Washington, D.C.

I was only seventeen.

Perfecting Nature

Once settled in at Georgetown, I began my studies in the pre-med program. Even though I was told that university work would be hard, I surprised everyone including myself with how quickly and easily I learned. I graduated from Georgetown *summa cum laude*, at the very top of my class. I had barely turned twenty-one.

That fall I entered medical school at Johns Hopkins University in Baltimore, Maryland. After having earned my medical degree and true to my original plan, I entered seminary training in my late twenties. I was ordained a Roman Catholic priest four years later. I managed to do this while also working toward a doctorate at Johns Hopkins.

My Ph.D. was in genetics. This, as well as my medical degree, grew out of my association with Tony—or, more specifically, out of those four pairs of pigeons he brought me from New York City. Darwin had spent years studying pigeons to understand how animal genes work, and now I wanted to follow in Darwin's footsteps.

I had learned from my reading of Darwin that through selective breeding I could heighten certain characteristics and suppress others. I also knew that if I simply left the birds to mate on their own, the purity of each variety would be lost, that in a few generations they would revert to looking like the motley pigeons I'd been keeping before Tony brought me the fancy breeds.

Over time, they'd become indistinguishable from street pigeons. This is because no matter how rare and distinctive certain breeds are—tumbling in mid-air or having fan-like tails or crests and little bows—they all are descendants of the wild originals, the kind that spend their time begging for crumbs in parks and perching on telephone wires. The wonders that can be developed with human intervention and selective breeding over time are always lost when Nature takes over.

Sometimes *perfection* demands more than Nature—it needs the intervention of human intelligence and human art.

Throughout my years of pursuing an advanced education in America I was able to finagle permission to install a coop on the roof of wherever I was living at the time, from freshman dorm to graduate student housing to the rambling rectory I shared with a few other young priests. This allowed me to conduct my own experiments while pursuing my studies. I know this sounds irregular—and it was. Eventually I acquired a reputation as "that eccentric young priest with the pigeons," but I didn't care.

In fact, I rather liked the distinction.

The Council and Modernity

I had promised my order that, in return for allowing me to pursue my doctorate, I would organize the Newman Club for Catholic students at Johns Hopkins and act as chaplain to the sick and dying at the university hospital. This was just a few years after the close of Vatican II.

Until that point I believed that I understood the great promise of America. Where else but in America could a foreigner, a stranger like me, be welcomed—and encouraged—to become all that I can be? For America told me, "If you are smart, if you work hard, if you do your utmost best, there's nothing—nothing—you cannot accomplish! So, think for yourself, be what you will, and prosper!"

Where else but here, in America, was there so much freedom to speak, to think, to act, and to pursue the truths of science wherever they might lead?

I had been thrilled to see all these things in the teachings of Vatican II: liberty of conscience, toleration, respect for science. It was truly an opening up of the human spirit, and it looked ever so much like the America I loved from the moment I set foot on her land.

But the Council also took the less admirable aspects of America and *magnified* them: rootlessness, the belief that the new is superior to the old, which translated into a veneration of youth, and ignorance of the truths, value, and beauty of history and culture.

I first noticed this at the hospital. In its efforts to liberalize and modernize the Church, the Council swept clean so much that had preceded it. But the old folks—men whose friends had passed, widows whose children no longer visited—needed stability and comfort, not "progress." So much that had given them a sense of order, purpose, and belonging throughout their lives—a neighborhood, family and friends, cultural and religious customs, even their health—was eroding away. Daily Mass was often the only thing they had left to count on and look forward to, and now even that had changed.

An earlier meaning of the English word "comfort" was "strength." And so my small disobedience to the Church's new directions was to comfort—to strengthen—my flock at the hospital by performing the rituals and religious customs that meant so much to them. On the theological level, Vatican II was correct. On the human level, it was often too painful, particularly to those who could least understand it.

It was, however, my association with the Newman Center that ultimately tainted how I viewed America and the effects of Vatican II.

The center was meant to be a haven for Catholic youth as they try to make their way in a non-Catholic, indeed non-religious world, with all its chaos and temptation.

But many, perhaps even most, of the students supposedly under my care had made their peace with the secular world. I was, to them, both foreign and antique. They knew little about Church history and even less about dogma and theology. Nor did they seem even slightly interested. It wasn't only difficult Catholic concepts such as transubstantiation but ordinary Christian concepts such as sin and temptation and the presence of Satan that they regarded as mumbo jumbo. The true religious spirit of the age was the spirit of Woodstock, and my students absorbed and reveled in it. Any notion that the mind, or the mind and the soul, should rule *over* the body was odd, even foreign, to them.

This manifested itself most clearly in the very thing I and my elderly friends at the hospital loved most: the Mass.

The Masses at the Newman Center (as, indeed, in so many contemporary parishes) were raucous affairs. Often the congregation sang and held hands or slowly waved their arms in the air. In some churches, the congregations sang loud and banal songs to guitar strumming, performed "liturgical dances," even pretended that they could speak in tongues! It was hard to tell such services from a loud and feverish Pentecostal prayer meeting.

These liturgical circuses made the cardinal error of mistaking the emotional *for* the spiritual. Congregations seemed to feel that the louder they sang, the more they swayed, the harder they wept or shouted out testimony, the closer they came to God. But they were only doing something physical, something emotional. They were, in fact, doing the exact opposite of a spiritual act—they were fully physical, fully bodily, sometimes, it seemed, fully brutish. At some Newman Center services, I often witnessed students work themselves into a frenzy. When their enthusiasm subsided, they would proclaim they'd had a deeply "religious" experience. But true spirituality floods the soul with light. Emotionalism is counterfeit spirituality—it only floods the body with excitement.

And so, I grew more and more to love the old Mass because the old Mass—performed in a dead language with set rules—cut the legs out from under such embarrassing giddiness.

It wasn't long before I left the Newman Center. I told my superiors that I was reaching a critical stage in my studies. This was true, although not the whole truth. Leaving gave me more time to devote to my new old friends at the hospital—and to my experiments.

My Brave New World

D espite the fact that I was still a priest, I increasingly saw myself as a physician and scientist. At Johns Hopkins, I was free to follow my deep interest in genetics—especially, in time, genetic engineering. To be able to transfer and reproduce certain traits in pigeons through selective mating was one thing. But to be able physically to remove genes from one organism and transfer them into another, *and then have that recipient organism make the transferred characteristics its own*, brought me exactly to where I had long hoped to be: able to use Science to manipulate and reproduce the magic of Creation!

I admit that, to the casual observer, my life might seem an ongoing paradox: priest, physician; lover of tradition, lover of liberty; humble farm boy, progressive scientist. But there was a unifying focus hidden in all of this.

For everything in my career had something to do with *life*, heavenly and, especially, earthly. Everything connected with life—its origins, its development, and its perfection—has, for as far back as I can remember, perplexed and fascinated me.

Along with so many of my fellow scientists, I thought

of Darwin as perhaps the greatest genius since Newton or Galileo. Like Darwin, my fellow biologists were fixated on the question of the origin of species and on evolution—that is, how is it that life has, through natural selection, evolved into different kinds. I, too, entered the field with this viewpoint.

But evolution and the work of natural selection is only a part of the true question—the question of life itself and with it the meaning of its perfection. Why, for example, in the midst of so much inanimate matter—air, stones, dirt, water—is there matter that has something clearly nonphysical, something spiritual, attached to it or infused into it that makes it animate, able to move from place to place, able even to reproduce itself? Or, at the highest level, able to allow it to have "thoughts"—things so obviously *nonmaterial* that it even seems odd to call a thought a "thing."

And how is it that when *life* leaves the body of even the highest and most intelligent organism, the body itself then becomes mere matter, never again able to live unless mystically "resurrected"—reanimated and ensouled, rejoining once again the world of Life. And while genetic engineering might never hope to transfer the mind or the soul, it might well be able to move certain qualities to the living even from the dead. Not now, perhaps not soon, but someday.

I found the mystery of the animation of matter by being permeated with some kind of soul or spirit so captivating that theology became, for me, the sister study of my work in biology and genetics. God is spirit without body. Matter is body without spirit. But living creatures are spirit and matter entwined. How is this even possible? And not only possible, but *actual*, and so actual that this animated, en-souled matter in humans enables us to cogitate on what has been thus divinely done.

To discover the full explanation, I knew I would need not only to pursue a science of life but also a science, a knowledge, of God. And here's where being a priest fit in, especially those years I spent on pure theological studies. Those studies, plus my study of philosophy and dabbling in the mystics and sages of the East, I felt, made my mind and my world whole.

It was a brave new world that could not be further re-moved from the simple world of my origins, among the olive trees and goats in the fields of Calabria.

Balthasar Castellani: Priest and Scientist

Thus far I've allowed Father Balthasar to speak in his own words. But to understand all that has happened, to grasp all the horrors he helped bring about, I must take up where the youthful Balthasar left off.

May God grant me the capacity to write it all out exactly as it has unfolded.

By the time he was in his early forties Father Balthasar could surely lay claim to being one of the best educated, even brilliant, of men. John Paul II was the first pope both to recognize as well as reward Balthasar's many special gifts. He invited Father to be one of his personal physicians and to serve as director of the Vatican's Academy of Science as well as curator of the Shroud of Christ in the cathedral in Turin. Popes Benedict, Francis, and later Clement XV, successor to the ill-fated Francis, followed John Paul's lead.

From the first, it was clear that his appointment as

curator of the Shroud held great importance to Father Balthasar as scientist *and* priest. He often remarked that it was this connection with the burial cloth of Christ Himself, and with the image imbedded in it, that was a highpoint of his most rich and full life. It was also this connection that ultimately brought about his downfall and so much of the destruction that has followed.

Good Works and Intentions

Despite the involved responsibilities of his appointments as physician, director, and curator, Father Balthasar's actual *pastoral* duties within the Vatican were simple. He was appointed confessor and spiritual director to an order of nuns living in a small convent near his office. It was at the Convent of St. Paul where Father often heard confessions, said daily Mass, and helped cultivate the good sisters' spiritual life.

It was a pleasant arrangement since Balthasar, who was by nature little given to small talk or banter, was lifted by the lightheartedness of the nuns, their charity, optimism, and simplicity. It filled a need for fellowship and doing the kind of good work he had left behind at the hospital in America. And the cheeriest nuns reminded him of Meg, whom he had never forgotten.

Even as he had grown in scientific erudition, Balthasar retained many of the austere habits of a priest. Other than his books, he owned very little, and never considered himself poor, since physically he needed almost nothing.

After John Paul invited him to join the Vatican staff, the good priest kept up the ascetic and scholarly life he lived in America. Living and working within the walls of the Vatican, Balthasar kept a small office piled floor to ceiling with his books. He took his meals with Father Adrian, his assistant, twice a day at the refectory, also located in the Academy. Yes, he appreciated good food and drink, but perhaps less than most other Italians. To be sure, he loved Sundays and feast days, when there might be chicken or a roast. But he also didn't mind Lent and Advent, when the fare was largely beans and bread, and even of that very little.

The Vatican owned most of Balthasar's scientific equipment. It was all housed in the Academy, as well as in his small laboratory, so he had easy and constant access to it. Next to his laboratory he had a small chapel, which was furnished with little more than a wooden kneeler and crucifix.

Balthasar owned a few black suits and shirts fitted with the usual Roman collars. In one of his few concessions to vanity, he kept a fine collection of beautiful silk vestments for saying Mass—scarlet for Pentecost and the great feasts of martyrs, purple and rose for penitential seasons, green for ordinary Sundays, pure white for most saints' days, and white with gold embroidery for high feasts such as Christmas and Easter.

After so many years away, being back in Italy also gave Balthasar an easy way to visit the farm, his family, and the Rizzos. He sometimes left it to Father Adrian to say daily Mass for the nuns, and headed down to offer Mass at the old family chapel, the one where, it was said, his father sheltered Jews during the war. Balthasar was also called back to the farm for longer periods, first for his mother's funeral and then, not three months later, the burial of his father.

They were interred in the unadorned plot next to the chapel.

While the loss of his parents grieved him deeply, the death of Tony Rizzo struck even deeper. Tony and Meg never had children, and the young Balthasar was raised by them as much as if not more than his natural parents. Their love for him was deep and palpable. They treated him not formally, but with hugs and carries and jostles and smiles. They treated him, Balthasar imagined, as good American parents would have.

So, when he got word of the Major's passing a year after his father died, Balthasar returned to the little stone cottage the Rizzos called home for more than thirty years. From there he accompanied Meg with Tony's body back to New York City.

He had asked for and gotten permission to have Tony's funeral mass said in St. Patrick's Cathedral. Except for Meg, no one grieved harder than Balthasar.

During Tony's funeral Balthasar looked over at Meg and thought back to his childhood, which was thoroughly Catholic. His family had attended Mass every Sunday, and observed every holy day, with fasting, almsgiving, and family prayer a regular part of daily life. Meg and Tony were observant Catholics, too, but they seemed to wear their faith more lightly; and yet it seemed to give them more joy than Balthasar saw at home.

"Why," a ten-year-old Balthasar once asked, "do I never see you praying? At home, we pray all the time."

"Oh, sweetheart," Meg responded, "we pray all the time, too."

"When? I never hear you. Mama asks God every day to help her. Papa, too."

"And does God answer her prayers?"

"Yes. I think so. Sometimes."

"And when He doesn't, are we sad, or disappointed?"

"Sure... I guess."

"Well, I don't think we should ever be disappointed with God. Let's look at prayer like this: God loves us, and knows everything. Does He really want us to beg Him for what we want when He knows even better than we do what we need? Since He loves us so immensely, He can be trusted to be on our side always. He doesn't want us to beg, only to trust."

Few conversations in Balthasar's life ever made so deep or so lasting an impression on him as this one short talk with Meg.

Designs of the Father

As Balthasar first learned from Meg, most people *ask* God for something when they pray. They might ask for an affliction or trial to pass, for the restoration of a loved one's health, for something they want or think they need to have. As a priest, Balthasar even knew other priests who prayed for their favorite team's victory in soccer matches. Most people seemed to treat God like an all-powerful king who hears, and then grants or denies our petitions. But ever since his conversation with Meg, Balthasar refused to approach God that way.

Following Meg's example, Balthasar came to the conclusion that, since God is all-loving and all-knowing and all-powerful, why would you ever ask Him to do something that, in His infinite wisdom and goodness, He had not planned to do? No. All that he need do was share what was in his heart with God and say, "Thy will be done." All else seemed arrogance.

Nonetheless, if prayer is communication with God, then Balthasar prayed constantly. They were not the usual structured, formal prayers all Catholics learn by heart. Rather, they were *conversations* with God, conversations as one might have while walking with a good friend or a spouse. The way he remembered Meg and Tony talking.

As Balthasar got older, this running commentary took on a certain cast. More and more Balthasar seemed to be pointing out to God how the world He had created really was a Cosmos. How everything in it fit together, how everything in it led to something else. Indeed, how intelligent and intelligible, how very rational God's creation was. Even evolution, about which Balthasar had no doubt, simply proved how all of creation worked together and ended exactly—*exactly*—where God intended.

It was this evidence of a stupendous Designer and a great design—this interconnectedness and rationality—that Balthasar discussed with God constantly. Above all, Balthasar thanked Him for the glory of the sensible world and for man's ability—especially for Balthasar's ability—to sense it.

This was how he knew for certain that he, Balthasar, was created in God's image, for even he, puny and insignificant in the universe's great scheme of things, could see the Cosmos in a small way as God saw it. He could understand with his own intelligence the Intelligence that had made this just so.

The First Thread Unravels

Secure that all was in his assistant Adrian's capable hands at the Vatican, Father Balthasar Castellani spent a full week during the winter of 2006 in Turin. It was time to consult with the archbishop of Turin and the priests of the cathedral who were keepers of the Holy Shroud. There had recently been a small fire in the church and, while the Shroud seemed well protected, it was time for a thorough review not only of the Shroud itself but also of its care and safety.

Balthasar had the Shroud taken down from its place of honor above the high altar in the chapel. It was removed from its silver casket and transferred, accompanied by a watchful assistant, the aged Father Pedro, to the small, well-equipped laboratory that had been set up in the chapel basement.

The two priests carefully unfolded the Shroud and set it out on the table. Father Balthasar leaned forward. "I need to take a closer look. Father Pedro, can you get the stronger magnifying glass I brought with me from Rome? I think it's in the leather bag I left in the sacristy."

"Ah, yes, Father, I'll go and fetch it."

Father Balthasar stood up and watched the elderly priest shuffle away, pulling the heavy laboratory door shut behind him. A far-off yet intense look took over the priest's face as he turned and looked down to study the ancient, unique length of cloth stretched out before him. Glancing back at the door, he removed a small vial and a pair of tweezers hidden in his lab coat pocket. Then in one swift movement, Balthasar opened the vial, leaned forward to pluck a few fibers from the cloth and place them in the vial, capping and returning it and the tweezers, his hands trembling slightly, to his lab coat pocket.

Father Balthasar stood up and slowly exhaled. He turned to face the door. "There you are, Father Pedro!" he said, his smile warm. "Let's begin, shall we?"

Father Adrian

Father Adrian Faulkner was ten years younger, almost to the day, than Father Balthasar, but at well over six feet, nearly a foot taller. In counterpoint to Balthasar's head of sparse, curly white hair, Adrian combed his thin, steel-gray hair straight back, which suited his longish face and angular features.

Though tall and lean, Adrian had the physical strength of two men. He had spent a few years in the Royal Navy, distinguishing himself as a boxer as well as a seaman. These physical qualities, in addition to an extremely sharp mind, improbably salty language, and deep interest in religious matters made Adrian stand out as a singular personality among his Vatican peers.

If Father Balthasar was short and round, and on the side of cheerful, Adrian was stern, almost severe. He came by it naturally. Born in England to an English father and Scottish mother, the family on both sides had always been staunch Roman Catholics. During the Reformation in England, Adrian's ancestors were burned alive for their steadfastness in the Faith. He had other ancestors who had been hanged until not quite dead, then saved from the gibbet only to be disemboweled while still breathing, all for God's sake. Adrian knew what untamed religious passion looked like, and he despised it.

In this sense, Adrian and Balthasar were of one mind. They found the idea that anyone would kill for God, or kill for religion, irrational, insane. The God of all humanity is a God of love, a God of peace. Yet, here's where they diverged. Balthasar's natural kindliness led him to believe that his dreams were true—that, nowadays at least, all serious religions pray to the same God, are essentially peaceful, and committed to toleration and religious freedom. True, here and there some hotheads may have "hijacked" their religion, but that didn't really change the fact that no one could truly give himself to God without seeing that God demands humility and love.

Meanwhile, Adrian—who growing up had seen firsthand in England the antagonism between Muslim Pakistanis and Hindu Indians, and even worse, the visceral hatred among Muslim youth of his generation for all things "Western," "Christian," and "modern"—held no romantic notions of the peacefulness of all religions. Some religions (and he had Islam particularly in mind) were little more than warlike cults of sexually charged ruffians who found in their religion a fitting excuse for their bloodlust.

As a parish priest in downtown London, Father Adrian had witnessed the rallies in Piccadilly Circus and Trafalgar Square, where young men whose supposed "love of God" led them to wave signs proclaiming "Behead Those Who Insult Islam," and "Butcher Those Who Mock the Prophet." Adrian had heard such protestors call non-Muslims, especially Jews, "pigs" and "apes" so often that he knew they were serious.

Adrian recognized that Islam today was where Europe had been four hundred years earlier, when his ancestors were being dismembered and torched for their beliefs. And yet the Christian sects in his native land, coming to see the wickedness of killing one another over dogmatic beliefs, had resigned themselves to differ peacefully on even the most essential matter: how to gain eternal life. But Islam was enflaming the youth of the world by promising not only a struggle here on Earth—a struggle that gave them a feeling of living life at its peak—but an afterlife of the most sumptuous and degraded sensual pleasure they could hope to imagine.

Adrian understood that Christian martyrs had suffered and died for their faith. But, today, only Islam among the world's major religions seemed to confer its highest honor not only on those who die but on those who kill—slaughtering women in the marketplace, children on playgrounds, innocent travelers on planes. Such murderers were seen as Islam's martyrs, as the holiest of God's creatures. Father Adrian found this fanaticism despicable and revolting.

He also found it impossible to constrain himself. At Mass, Adrian's homilies became more and more political. His calls for good Christians to understand, defend, and fight for their faith—and for the Christian heritage of Europe as well—set him crosswise with his more tolerant and understanding bishop. So Adrian was transferred to the Vatican, where his talents, perhaps even his combativeness, might still serve Mother Church without causing needless turmoil.

In 2005, not long after our Holy Father John Paul's death, Adrian was assigned to the Vatican's Academy of Science, and became Father Balthasar's first and only assistant.

Adrian was immediately drawn to Balthasar's brilliance, especially in science and medicine. But more than that, he recognized that Balthasar was holy, a man in whom intelligence lived comfortably with simplicity and charity.

Their respect and affection for each other was evident from the first. And in their views of the Church, of science, and of modernity, Adrian and Balthasar were essentially of one mind. Yet they had one clear area of disagreement: Balthasar hated nothing in this world.

Adrian hated Islam.

Unholy Thursday

It was only by God's immortal grace and mercy that Sister St. Rose, shaken from having been attacked herself, managed to get Sister Maria Fidelis, still bleeding and senseless, into the car and drive, too shocked to cry or even pray, back to the Convent of St. Paul.

The authorities were never contacted. This would be at Sister Maria's unwavering insistence throughout her convalescence from the brutal rape, with Sister St. Rose's iron-jawed support. No amount of pleading that they had an obligation to other women to have the police find and incarcerate their attackers moved them.

Only when the two sisters were alone did they speak more freely. Sister St. Rose was angry and ashamed. "It's all my fault! If I hadn't wanted to sing in the choir that night, none of this would have happened." That Sister Maria kept repeating "But I insisted on staying to pray" unnerved and further distressed her. "A great part of virtue is prudence," Sister St. Rose finally blurted out. "Two young women walking a seedy neighborhood alone at night wasn't prudent!"

"Has not Christ told us all to forgive those who attack

us?" Sister Maria replied in a soft voice. "Was not infinitely worse done to Him, yet He forgave? When will we ever have such a chance to follow Our Lord's very words than right now?"

In response, Sister St. Rose could only take Sister Maria's hand and weep.

The Observation

From the first Sister Maria had been wildly adamant that the attack on her be reported no further, and Sister Margaret, the Mother Superior, had at last grudgingly agreed. However, she insisted on calling for Father Balthasar, who served as primary physician to the nuns of the convent. Mother Superior relied on him and never failed to follow whatever course he thought best.

Father Balthasar came alone to examine Sister Maria. Cut, bruised, and battered, she was extremely agitated by the attack. Above all things, she was terrified by the possibility that the rape would leave her pregnant.

Father Balthasar decided it was best to keep Sister Maria under observation. For nearly a week, he kept her alone and heavily sedated. During that week, Balthasar did something that he would decide to keep secret for most of the rest of his life.

Sister Maria Fidelis

With time to rest, Maria was moved to her convent cell. There, carefully watched over by Sister St. Rose, they were able to talk freely, and Sister Maria began to recover in body and spirit.

Throughout her recuperation there was no thought, on her part or anyone else's, that she would abort the child, if she were pregnant. But Sister Maria needed to know—the whole convent needed to know—the truth. Was there a child?

"For now, let us pray about it," advised Sister Margaret. "Father Balthasar will tell us soon enough."

As Maria recuperated, she reflected on all the implications of her rape while studying the walls of her convent cell. The convent was an old stone building built by the Knights Templar during the time of the Crusades. With the papal suppression of the Knights in the fourteenth century it was taken over by Augustinians, the same order of monks and priests who produced Martin Luther in Germany in the sixteenth century. In the nineteenth century, the monastery was converted into a convent for nuns connected with this same Augustinian order, and named the Convent of St.

Paul.

Eighteen other Augustinian nuns resided in the convent with Sister Maria, plus four nuns from the Sisters of Charity, the society founded by the sainted Mother Theresa. Sister Maria was among the youngest of the Augustinians, having been born and named Agnes twenty-two years before to a wealthy industrial family in Milan.

Prominent and worldly in fairly obvious ways, the Moretti family was also always rather religious. Agnes's father inherited the business, and ran it well, though he harbored thoughts that he might have made a decent priest, perhaps even a missionary. He attended Mass each morning in the great cathedral before heading to work.

Beautiful in that slender and stylish way only northern Italian women seem to have mastered, Agnes's mother was truly devout. It was she who saw to it that each Christmas a hundred thousand Euros found its way into the Church's coffers or the hands of the various social charities that fed the poor or cared for the sick or elderly.

Little Agnes Moretti knew she had a vocation to the religious life from the age of six. When twelve years later Agnes proclaimed that she would be entering a convent, there was none of the usual handwringing about how she would never raise a family or enjoy the comforts of the world. The Morettis fully acknowledged that in this life, all joys compete; one had to renounce some things to gain others. "If one must give up the world to gain the joy of closeness to God and the happiness of heavenly life," her mother declared when Agnes announced her vocation, "then that is a decision upon which both the head and the heart can agree."

And so, at eighteen, having given up all prospects of wealth and marriage, Agnes Moretti joyfully entered the Convent of St. Paul and became Maria Fidelis, the name she took for herself as a novice.

This combination of her father's faith, her mother's good works, and Agnes's prayers and devotion over the years meant that the Moretti family was pretty much assured of being together eternally in Heaven, before God.

Still, while Heaven might seem a far-off certainty, this life on Earth—with all its inherent uncertainties and sorrows, its joys and perhaps even horrors—still needed to be confronted. It was for strength in the face of Life that Maria prayed every day.

CONVERGENCE

Salvatore

Sister Maria went into labor in the early hours of January 20, 2010. Mother Superior and Sister Teresa of the Child Jesus were in the delivery room with Father Balthasar—though, if truth be told, Sister Teresa's only task was to hold Maria's hand, pray quietly, and put a comforting cool handkerchief to her forehead.

As the sun rose, the boy arrived. Much to everyone's relief, it was a surprisingly easy birth. Maria nursed the infant as soon as he was washed, crying not unhappy tears the entire time.

The introduction of the baby to the sisters of the convent took place that afternoon, and immediately the only issue was what to name the new child. Everyone had an opinion and everyone wanted a vote. Since January 20 was the feast of St. Sebastian, there was a strong contingent of pro-"Sebastian" supporters. Father Adrian, who had been taken into the convent's confidence regarding the child's origins, remarked it lucky he wasn't born a week later or the poor thing might have been saddled with the unfortunate name of "Polycarp." Sister Maria was partial to "Angelo," since, despite everything, he seemed a little angel.

Father Balthasar suggested they name the child "Salvatore," after Our Savior Himself. This had few supporters, until Mother Superior said that if that's what the good father wanted, that's what the child should be named, and everyone pretty much fell in line. Even Sister Maria agreed, so long as everyone promised not to shorten it to "Sal."

In point of fact, by the time Salvatore arrived Father Balthasar already had his first few years thought through. Since the Vatican was a separate, sovereign entity, not much had to be shared with any authorities outside its walls. The birth was not recorded. For all the world knew, Salvatore was a foundling left at the convent door. If anyone asked, it was guessed he was the child of one of the gardeners who was too poor to support another hungry mouth. Beyond the convent walls no one would ever know—no one needed to know—that Salvatore was Sister Maria Fidelis's child.

There was still an orphanage within the Vatican. Indeed, it was a rather thriving orphanage, if that's the right way to put it, with children who were abandoned, or the children of migrants who were unable to support them, or children whose parents were deceased. It was run by the Sisters of Mercy, who tried to place the infants with good families in Rome, though there were always more foundlings than were wanted elsewhere. The sisters kept a good home for the children who remained at the orphanage, loving and schooling them right there in the Vatican.

It was decided that, once weaned, Salvatore would reside at this orphanage rather than stay in the Convent of St. Paul. It was further decided that Father Balthasar would be in charge of his education, and that as soon as he had made his First Holy Communion, Salvatore would begin to spend time living, studying, and assisting Father Balthasar in the priests' residence nearby.

This was all extremely irregular, but Father Balthasar insisted; and everyone acknowledged that the continued proximity of Salvatore to Sister Maria Fidelis over the years would be a good and just thing—and the least that was due her, given her wrenching ordeal. She could never openly be Salvatore's mother in any typical sense, but she could now watch him grow, and thereby transform what originated in tragedy into something quite beautiful.

Salvatore was amazingly precocious. And so, Balthasar, with Adrian's assistance, began his education—a true education—before the boy even reached the age of four. First came the art of reading and languages, which he picked up with almost unnerving ease. Besides, of course, Italian, he had a facility with Latin and English by the time he was six. It was basic at first, but under the priests' careful tutelage Salvatore's reading and then writing skills flourished, and his spoken English, in particular, was superb.

In his other studies arithmetic quickly became mathematics, and with Balthasar's laboratory at hand, science was ever-present. Under Father Adrian's direction, other subjects completed Salvatore's school hours: literature of every kind, poetry and plays, universal history. When Salvatore turned nine he was introduced to philosophy—

logic, then epistemology, then metaphysics, then moral and political philosophy.

All of this, every bit of it, was overlaid with theology and liturgical studies. And it was in theology and related subjects that Salvatore truly excelled. He became Balthasar's acolyte as soon as he had made his Communion, and it was obvious to all that he loved nothing more than to serve at daily Mass, even though it meant getting up at 5:00 a.m. to assist Balthasar in celebrating the sacred liturgy at 6:00 at the convent for the sisters.

All of this was the loveliest and most satisfying arrangement that Balthasar, Sister Maria, and even Adrian could have ever envisioned.

Salvatore's Pigeons

Wherever he went, wherever he lived, Father Balthasar found a way to build a coop on the roof and keep a few pigeons. In coming to Rome, however, he had agreed to take on serious and varied responsibilities, and over time he began to despair of making room in his schedule to raise his beloved birds again. But once Salvatore turned eight—the same age he himself had been when, under Tony's tutelage, he started keeping pigeons in earnest—the hope of reconnecting with his childhood and his early life's work, and of offering the joy of it all to Salvatore, pushed aside Balthasar's concerns.

With the help of a Vatican custodian Balthasar built a small plywood coop. It had a slanted overhanging roof, nesting room for at least ten pairs of pigeons, and a screened-in area that could be opened for the birds to perch protected and preen in the sun. Short as he was, it still was too small for the good father to stand in, but just the right height for Salvatore. And if Salvatore took to it as he grew, they could build a larger coop in a few years.

After constructing the coop, Balthasar went into Rome, where he knew he could find the birds he sought. Balthasar had decided to forego the fanciest varieties—the fantails, jacobins, satinettes, and Oriental frills—in favor of more standard birds. He brought back two mated pairs of tumblers, and one pair of Modenas, the chunky, round, full-chested pigeons from northern Italy.

Once the birds had been set up with straw for bedding, feed, and clean water, Balthasar introduced Salvatore to the flock.

The boy, who usually got excited over every and any small thing, merely looked puzzled. "There are pigeons all over Rome. Why are we putting more of them on our roof?" he asked a stunned Balthasar.

"Look at how beautiful they are, Salvatore! And, in a few days, when they're accustomed to where they now live, we'll let them out and watch them fly. Then you'll see that they not only come home every time, but the four tumblers will do acrobatics as they land."

"Why?"

"Because it's in a pigeon's nature to be a homing animal. Some have the trait more than others, but all pigeons have it."

"No, why do they do acrobatics when they land?"

"Because this is where they live: they have food and water and a warm, comfortable nest. Pigeons are great show-offs. When they're happy, they do certain things, like acrobatics. It's only natural for a pigeon to want to be in his coop, happy, safe, and sound."

Salvatore seemed unconvinced. "But don't these pigeons want to fly with other pigeons and peck for food whenever they want and sleep wherever they want and be free—

free to do what God wants them to do, not what we'd like? Wouldn't that be more natural and make them happier?"

Trying to hide his disappointment at the boy's lack of enthusiasm, Balthasar was about to discourse on the many possible meanings of "natural," but checked himself. "Salvatore, you're the most philosophic eight-year-old I've ever known. Someday we'll have to talk about this more."

The Holy Shroud

As Science Director to the Vatican, Balthasar advised the Holy Father on virtually all scientific matters; he was privy to all papal pronouncements touching on scientific or technical affairs; and, as already noted, he was the pope's legate in full charge of the miraculous Shroud of Turin. More than anything else, it was this task, this responsibility, that gave Balthasar's life meaning and joy. Indeed, everything that made him a priest, a scientist, and a pilgrim to Heaven was wrapped up in this one glorious and sacred artifact.

The Shroud was believed by millions—and by no one more fervently than Balthasar—to be the cloth that covered Christ when He was taken down from the cross and laid in the tomb. It had impressed upon it the very picture of Christ Himself. It had the image of His whole body—His bruised face, His pierced hands and feet, the open wound in His side, the puncture holes in His scalp, the remnants of the scourging on His back, the twisted agony of His corpus, and, above all, the remnants of our Lord and Savior's bodily fluids and dried drops of His most precious blood.

Since 1578, the Shroud had been safeguarded in the

chapel of the Cathedral of Saint John the Baptist, the Duomo, in Turin, in northern Italy. But its history before that is unclear. Some sources show that it first appeared in Lirey, France, in 1353. There is, oddly, no mention of the Shroud anywhere in Europe before that date. It was first publically viewed elsewhere in France in 1357, so it appears that the Shroud was over 1300 years old before anyone—or at least, any Europeans—ever saw it. However, one tradition has it that the Shroud was stolen from Constantinople in 1204, where it had been entrusted since its removal from the Holy Land years earlier.

As one might imagine, this lack of careful, documented provenance cast real doubt on the authenticity of the Shroud, for why would anything so precious have no history, no solid record, for apparently thirteen centuries? Add to this that fake relics abounded in medieval Europe, and in Italy and France especially, so why wouldn't the Shroud also be a fake? Today tourists visit Rome to eat fried artichokes and *cacio e pepe* or tour the Coliseum and purchase the finest leather goods. But not so in ages past, when travelers to this once decayed and backward city came for one thing and one thing alone: to venerate relics and prostrate themselves before sacred icons. Of course, this meant that relic mongering and relic forgeries were rampant not only in the Eternal City but everywhere throughout the Christian world.

The Shroud's authenticity was even a source of some dispute between Balthasar and Adrian. The Shroud's lack of settled history and the possibility of forgery had always been enough to settle the matter for Adrian, the eternal skeptic.

"How could it be that such an important relic of Christ's burial would have been preserved by persons and in circumstances unknown to the Church? An object this sacred, the very form of the crucified Christ imprinted on a cloth saturated with His blood, and it's nowhere mentioned in a thousand years? It strains credulity, Balthasar. And for it to show its face, so to speak, just when the trade in holy relics is at a peak, when nothing would sell for more! I can't believe that a man of science such as you would believe the Shroud authentic. We both know that, as Catholics, we're called upon to believe a hell of a lot of very, very implausible things. Why add one more impossibility to the mix?"

To all this, Balthasar gave the orthodox response: "It was not uncommon for manuscripts, art, relics of various sorts to be kept in monasteries for centuries, while their true significance gradually drifted out mind. You know, Adrian, that the oldest complete copy of the New Testament—the *Codex Sinaiticus*—sat in a Sinai monastery for more than a thousand years. The monks knew it was worth keeping even if they had no idea how incredibly rare and valuable it was. My guess is that the Shroud was held in a venerable and safe spot in some hillside or desert monastery for hundreds of years before it was secretly brought to Constantinople, where they knew quite well what it was.

"Besides, it is exact and perfect—perfect beyond any art, perfect in every way. The wounds correspond exactly with the reported wounds of Christ: the beating with fists and blows to the face with a club, the flogging, the crown of thorns, the nailing of the hands and feet, the unbroken legs, the lance thrust to the side, and, after death, the flowing of blood and water from the side wound. It can be no one other than our Lord, Adrian, no one."

"Come on, Balthasar. Any decent painter with a sheet of linen and the Gospel text before him could do the same thing."

"No, Adrian. You know he couldn't. There's no paint, no pigment, no oils, no dyes anywhere on this Shroud. I don't know what caused this image to appear—the burial spices or the sacred, celestial energy that revivified Our Lord after three days or His will that we have His image to venerate forever—I really don't. And I'm saying this as a scientist: no one knows how the image was created. What we *do* know is that it's not a painting, it's not a rubbing, it's not anything that any scientist or artist can duplicate. And besides, what's on the cloth is real blood, Christ's blood, not paint."

Adrian shook his head. "I still don't believe it. And the only thing I would believe even less, Father, is if you told me it was a photograph that some first-century photographer developed on a piece of cloth. Now that would be a miracle!"

"You are such a cynic Adrian and sometimes I have no idea why I like you so much. Consider this: In all the paintings you've ever seen of the crucifixion by any artist painted in any century, how is Christ held to the cross?"

"By nails."

"Yes, Adrian, by nails. And where were these nails driven?"

"Into the hands and into the feet."

"Where in the hands?"

"In the palms of Christ's hands. Where else would they go?"

"You are correct, my brother Adrian, that's where every artist puts the nails, every single painter who's ever lived, in the palms of Christ's hands. But do you know where these nails shown on the Shroud were driven? Into the wrists! Take my word as a physician, a body would rip off the cross within minutes if hung by the palms of the hands. The Romans crucified people by nailing them through the wrists. So how did this mysterious medieval artist know enough to put the wounds through the wrists when not one single person in all of medieval Europe had any notion of how the Romans crucified people in first-century Palestine? A clairvoyant genius, this painter of yours! He uses paints and he guards secrets unknown to the rest of the world."

Adrian frowned, "Let me get this straight, Balthasar. When science can't prove it was Christ, and documentation and provenance fail you, you choose to rely on art history! Now do you see why I just can't buy it?"

"Buy it or not, Adrian, we have in our possession in Turin the burial cloth of Christ, the blood of Christ, and an image on it that has every detail perfect, including the one small detail, the wrists, of which no artist before or after him was aware."

Flight

Salvatore continued to assist with the care of Father Balthasar's beloved coop and training of its inhabitants, but in truth he and the pigeons never really got along. When the time came that Balthasar entrusted their care almost entirely to Salvatore, the boy would climb the steps to the roof after morning Mass to let the birds out and listlessly watch them fly about. If they looked like they were going too far afield, he'd shake the feed can and they'd return, wanting to eat. He'd toss two handfuls of feed into the coop, and as soon as the birds rushed in he quickly shut the coop door. Salvatore would stare at the door for a few moments before returning to his room to study or head for class with Father Adrian, trying not to give the pigeons another thought.

Unless someone else brought them up.

Nearly every year the good father attended a Church conference on genetics. Balthasar always enjoyed going; he learned much from other doctors, scientists, and prelates, and he definitely enjoyed their company.

Usually the conference was held someplace in Europe, but not this year.

"The meetings this year are in New York," he told Salvatore, as they stood with Father Adrian, waiting for his taxi to the airport. "It's a city I haven't been to in years and I'm so very much looking forward to going. I'm certain you'll take as good care of the pigeons as I would, my boy. You will have to tell me all about their activities when I return."

"The pigeons will be fine," Father Adrian chided with a laugh. "Here's your ride. We'll see you when you get back." Adrian and Salvatore waved as Father Balthasar's taxi pulled away and expertly dove into the crowded, unpredictable Roman traffic.

On their walk back to the refectory for lunch, Adrian attempted to make small talk, but Salvatore was thoughtful. While Adrian himself had absolutely no use for pigeons, he felt it right to ask. "So, do you like the pigeons Father bought for you?"

"I guess so." Salvatore's voice was uncharacteristically hesitant.

"*Hmm.* Is that an 'I guess so' yes or an 'I guess so' no?"

"Well, they're... okay," Salvatore replied. Then he volunteered an observation. "They actually look kind of sad. Like they want to be with the other pigeons that just fly around and be birds—not pets all caged up and forced to entertain us. I told Father Balthasar that it didn't seem right to coop them up like that! I think they want to be with their own kind, and have friends. He said we'd talk about it, but we never have."

Adrian decided not to press further after that comment, but a few days later he inquired about how things were going in the coop, adding, "The question I asked you the other day, Salvatore, was whether *you* like the pigeons, not whether *they* are happy."

"Oh. Well, I guess I like them enough," said Salvatore, staring out the window. "Feeding them and letting them fly around, and getting them to go back in the coop isn't that hard. The only part I really didn't like was scraping the coop."

"*Didn't* like? Have you stopped cleaning it?"

"Well, yes. The custodian who helped Father Balthasar build the coop—you know him, his name is Luca—asked to see the pigeons one day. So I said he could see them as often as he liked if he'd clean the coop. Otherwise, no."

"I wonder what Father Balthasar will think about this, Salvatore."

"Please don't tell him. Please?"

Salvatore was asking, but Father Adrian noticed a hint of steely defiance in the boy's tone that made him uneasy.

Reunion

During his flight to New York Balthasar thought about how he wasn't looking forward to the conference as much as the opportunity attending it gave him to see Meg. They hadn't seen one another since that rainy, cheerless day they buried Tony.

Skipping one afternoon of meetings, Balthasar took the Metro-North train to a nursing home on the eastern shore of Westchester County, to a facility on a cliff overlooking the magnificent Hudson River. He was delighted to find Meg eagerly expecting him.

"Oh, Balthasar, I've missed you something terrible!" she said, reaching up to embrace him. "I was afraid I'd die without seeing you again. Writing letters and talking on the phone just aren't the same as being together. I know how busy you are, and I can't tell you how glad I am you're here."

At the age of ninety-two, Meg was wheelchair-bound, but her eyes were as clear and her mind as sharp as ever. And it was obvious from their discussion over tea that Meg's loving heart was bursting with joy and a kind of motherly pride.

"I try to follow news stories about you," she said. "You're

very famous, you know. The last big thing I saw was an interview you gave about your visit to Turin to examine the Shroud. You told the world that it was in excellent condition for something nearly two thousand years old. You defended its authenticity so passionately that I'm sure everyone who saw it was persuaded. I know I was!" Meg put her hand on her heart. "I'm so proud that Tony and I know you. Does this conference you're attending have to do with the Shroud?"

"Oh, no, dear Meg," Balthasar replied, touched by Meg's habit of referring to her beloved husband in the present tense. "It's a yearly conference I attend on genetics that the Church convenes. I would much rather it was as you said, however. The field of genetics moves so fast that half the time I sit bewildered at what's being argued at the sessions." Balthasar leaned forward to add in a whisper, "But please don't tell our Holy Father that," and they both chuckled.

Meg reached out and patted Balthasar's hand. "Tony and I take such joy in all you've allowed God to make of you. Do you have any idea how much we love you?"

"I do," Balthasar responded, reddening. "And I hope you know how much I love you."

Meg smiled.

"But it's easy to love you and Tony," Balthasar continued. "I think every day of all you did for me—all the trust you placed in me." His voice faltered. "But why do you love *me* so much? You have always loved me as if I were your own child."

"Balthasar, we love you more even than that! It's natural

to love one's own. But Tony and I willed to love you because of what we saw in you—let's call it goodness and intelligence mixed seamlessly together. Philosophers say that the love of human excellence is the peak of human love. We see that in you; we always have."

Here Meg squeezed Balthasar's hand and studied his face, which seemed to compel her to say more. "Our love for you also leads us to worry about you. Your letters and calls in recent years seem to carry a sadness. I sense some burden is weighing you down. I can see it in your eyes right now."

Balthasar sat up and looked away. "Oh, Meg, I'm sure it's just the worry that I might never see you again. It's become such a heaviness that even being here with you today can't overcome it."

The Sadness of Civilization

On the afternoon of his return from the genetics conference Father Balthasar got settled in, and then, hoping to find Salvatore, immediately went up to the roof to check on the pigeons. Instead he discovered a bare, open coop.

Balthasar found Salvatore with Adrian, doing a lesson on Ancient Rome.

Adrian welcomed Balthasar into the room with a wave. "Good see you, Father Balthasar. How was the conference?"

Adrian was surprised by the abrupt response. "It was fine. Father, may I borrow Salvatore for a minute?"

Salvatore couldn't help but notice the priest's countenance and tone. "Forgive me, Father, I know you're angry with me."

"What happened to the lovely pigeons I bought, Salvatore?"

"Oh, Father, I could tell by their eyes how sad they were! So the other day I fed them *before* I sent them off to fly and they were so full of joy that they kept going and going. I think they were happy to be free. I left the door to the coop open because you told me pigeons always return home when they can. When they never returned, I realized they had found new homes, and were finally happy to be themselves."

Balthasar's voice was quiet. "In no time they'll wind up as food for cats or be ripped apart by hawks. Do you think that will make them happy?"

"I don't know, Father. Do you think God is happy that we have made these living things after our own fancy instead of enjoying to see them as God Himself had made them?"

"I think God wants us to do all we can with His creation," Father Balthasar answered firmly, "to make it more productive, more interesting, more useful, and even more beautiful. This is why God our Father gave humanity stewardship over all creation. With our knowledge we can make the world better, lovelier—"

"Why?" Salvatore interrupted, in a voice neither priest had heard him use before. "Is our created world more lovely than God's natural world? How is it that the birds that please us with their acrobatics are lovelier than the birds that fly close to God and flap their wings with joy at all He has done for them?"

Father Balthasar had no words to respond to Salvatore, who continued in a tone, despite his youth, that ended the discussion. "I'm sorry I've displeased you, Father. I knew I would. But I thought releasing the pigeons from our prison and letting them be all that God made them to be was right and just."

Father Balthasar didn't know whether to be impressed, or worried.

The Second Incarnation

In October 2020, on the evening of the twelfth day, Adrian poked his head into Father Balthasar's room. "Have a sip of port you might care to share?"

"Of course!" Balthasar replied with a friendly wave—as he always did. "Come in, dear Adrian. Let's have a small drink and talk."

Adrian smiled and watched as Balthasar walked over in his slippers to the corner table that held the alcohol. He walked with his usual sprightly gait—sprightly for a man in his seventies—but Adrian noticed that Balthasar slowed down as he approached the table. And that Balthasar hesitated before extending his hand to grasp the bottle. And that Balthasar stood there, staring at the bottle for far too long before coming back to the moment to pour two drinks.

"Are you alright, Father?"

"Just thinking, Adrian. Just thinking." Balthasar looked as if he were about to re-cork the bottle, but then he poured another half-inch to top off each glass.

"We've now known each other for many years, my friend," Balthasar began, handing Adrian a glass. "We've had many serious conversations, many of them in this room, over a small drink. Philosophy, theology, science... You know my mind pretty well and I think I know you as deeply as I've ever known anyone. But there's something I've never told you, something I think you should know. It's actually quite important, but I've kept it secret for years."

Adrian set down his glass. "Is this a confession, Father? Shall I—"

"No, Adrian, it's not like that. It's odd, and I wonder if you'll think me mad—but it's not a sin. I don't believe it's a sin..." Balthasar's voice trailed away. And then he resumed speaking, plowing forward with resolve. "For reasons you'll soon see, I've never told this to another soul. Nor would I. Ever. It concerns me and it concerns Salvatore."

"Father!"

"Adrian, let me finish. No, I mean let me start. We both know how bright Salvatore is. I'm not going to flatter you by saying it's your teaching, Adrian. What you, or we, have been able to bring out of that boy is nothing short of marvelous, but he seems to be a genius—no, more than a genius. He does seem to grasp things intuitively, no?"

Adrian, relieved, could only nod.

Balthasar set down his drink and began to pace. "What I mean is that Salvatore learns things by sight, and often just by hearing them once. He grasps ideas, theological concepts, languages, everything. Do you not think there's something fantastic about him?"

"Of course, Father, of course," Adrian agreed. "He could apply himself more to math and science, but he knows some things at ten that took me until I was thirty years old to understand. He has amazing facility."

Balthasar's nodded in vigorous agreement. "Remember how Jesus was left behind in Jerusalem when he was almost as young as Salvatore? When Mary and Joseph found him, Jesus was in the temple conversing with the rabbis. They were 'astonished,' St. Luke says, astonished at all the boy knew and could explain. Does that not remind you of Salvatore?"

"Salvatore may be brilliant but he's certainly not—"

Balthasar cut Adrian off. "*He is.* That's exactly, *exactly*, who he is."

"This verges on blasphemy!" Adrian cried. "Salvatore may be a genius, but he's not the equivalent of Our Lord."

Balthasar sighed, and held out his hand, as if to ward off Adrian's reaction. "Here's what you don't know, my dear Adrian, what no one knows. A few years before Sister Maria was attacked, I was in Turin, in my capacity as overseer of the Shroud. It was time to do a full examination of the sacred fabric."

"Of course, Balthasar, I know. It's something you do every few years, to ensure there's no deterioration, no change in the cloth."

"Yes, but that year I felt compelled to do something... something highly irregular. I brought with me a perfectly clean vial, a sterile vial, and tweezers, also sterile. And when I was alone in the room I pulled a few fibers from the Shroud—fibers with grains of Christ's blood on them—and deposited them in the vial, which I took with me."

Adrian sat back in his chair.

"I knew the Church, the world, might see it as sacrilegious, but I saw it as scientifically necessary. If anything ever happened to the Shroud, at least these fibers would be saved. Once I got back here, to my lab, I examined the blood—type AB, fairly rare—and separated the DNA from the sample. Then I saved the DNA. It was completely uncontaminated. I had it sealed and discretely labeled.

Balthasar took a long sip of port before resuming his story. "But by my honor until that fateful moment, when all was revealed to me, I had no idea of the true purpose behind what I had done and what I was compelled to do!"

"What the hell are you talking about, Balthasar?"

"Everything could have been left the way it was," Balthasar mused. "God forgive me, I know that, Adrian. But I also felt that He would direct me to take further action. Why and to what end, in His wisdom, I did not know; so, for the time being I safeguarded the sample of Our Lord Jesus Christ's DNA in my lab.

"Not long after this I was in my chapel, meditating on a few passages in Second Peter: 'Conduct yourselves in holiness and devotion, and wait for and hasten the coming of the day of God.' I asked what could this mean—What could I do to 'hasten' our Lord's Second Coming? And He said to me as clearly as He has ever spoken to me, Adrian. 'I need you to be wakeful and watchful, and you will soon see—and act.'"

"What did you do, Balthasar?"

"God's words ran through me like an electric current, Adrian. There was a plan for me! As with Mary, who was chosen to bring into the world Our Lord's first incarnation, I was part of God's plan, a plan to help bring about Christ's return. I had no idea what that meant, until that Holy

Thursday, when Sister Maria returned to the convent, having been brutally—"

Adrian rose to his feet, but Balthasar held out his hand.

"I must finish this, old friend. Yes, it wasn't until Mother Superior led me in the darkness of night into that room where Maria lay, bruised and weeping and—transformed—that I knew what I was called upon to do. I knew it fell to me to take the purified genetic essence of Our Lord that I had taken from the Shroud and infuse it into the embryo in Maria. With God's help, I knew that the child Maria would bear would be Christ Himself—yes, Christ revivified."

Adrian couldn't move.

"So, it's not simply that Salvatore 'reminds' me of Christ," Balthasar exclaimed. "Salvatore IS Christ."

The Serpent Voice

Adrian stood there, pale and shaking. "Let me get this straight. You took genetic material from the Shroud, material that you *think* contains Christ's DNA, and inserted whatever the hell it is into the fetus growing inside Sister Maria?"

His voice trailed off, then boomed out. "You did this to that poor woman after she was raped? How could you—and how did you even do it? Did you somehow exchange the fetal DNA for the DNA you gathered?"

"Please, Adrian, don't shout," Balthasar urged. "Let us speak calmly and rationally, as friends and scientists. No, in my lab I'm hardly equipped to do such work. To be certain, I hesitated. I even told our Father what He of course knew—that genetic transfers are infinitely more complicated and difficult than this. But He simply said that He was calling on me to obey, and that I should put my trust in Him. If I obeyed, He said, together we would bring all things to fruition. So, trusting in His infinite love, I put aside my hesitation and followed where I was led. I followed the commands I was given, Adrian—the commands I *know* I was given. God would, and now I know God did, take over from there."

Adrian shook his head wildly. "I'm trying hard to understand, Balthasar. You tell me that you took foreign material, *stolen* foreign material, and inserted it into the child growing in Maria's womb. Her body, having been violated, you thought it acceptable for you to violate it once more! You did this because you heard a voice. You did this because you're convinced that it's Christ's blood on that shroud. And you tell me you did this because you believe that God was asking for *your assistance* in returning Our Lord to Earth?" Adrian's breath was ragged. "You want to know what I think? I think you're fucking INSANE!"

"Don't speak that way, Adrian!" Father Balthasar cried. "You of all people, I thought, would understand that I seek fellowship, not condemnation, in sharing my story. You know that everything I have ever experienced, everything I have ever studied, everything that I believe, led me to such action. *It all fits together perfectly.*"

Adrian waved his hands, as if to ward away Balthasar's argument.

"Don't you see, Adrian? This is why God impelled me to study all I have over the years. And it's why He pushed me to take the vial to Turin. To hasten Our Lord's return is the reason I was born, the reason I was put on Earth. It's not madness—it's God's will."

"Father, this is madness. You *say* you heard God's voice. And you fancy that voice called you to imitate the Holy Spirit and play God—that you would be the agent in bringing Christ back to life. You've followed the path of so many others who bring grief into this world: *You find in Scripture what you want to find and you think God talks especially to you.* You're not just a madman, you're an arrogant, prideful madman."

Balthasar recoiled as if struck.

Though merely a growl, Adrian's voice filled the room. "You thought you would take upon yourself to act like God and bring Jesus back to life. Do you recognize your blasphemy, Balthasar? You fancy it was God speaking to you when it was the Serpent's voice. *'Commanded by God to act'*? That's what every lunatic says!"

Balthasar only raised his chin for reply.

Adrian threw his hands in the air. "You've committed a crime, Balthasar, the penance for which I can't even begin to imagine. You once told me that you never ask God for anything, but now you'd better start. Start praying that God forgives you—then ask for the strength you'll need to survive the tragedy I'm certain you've brought on. For my part, I'm going now to pray—for you, for Maria, for Salvatore, perhaps for all of us."

Adrian strode toward the door, but paused with his hand on the doorknob. "'Conduct yourselves in holiness and devotion, and wait for and hasten the coming of the day of God.' If you think you've found license in Scripture for with what you've done, Balthasar, you should sit with the words in Second Peter that follow—'hasten the coming of the day of God *when the heavens will be dissolved in flames and the elements melted by fire.*'"

The Angel in the Garden

O n an unseasonably warm Saturday afternoon in early spring 2021, Sister Maria Fidelis and Sister St. Elizabeth, an expert gardener visiting from the Convent of the Holy Cross in downtown Rome, had come into the herb garden, where shoots of tarragon and mint were already flourishing in the carefully tended soil.

Salvatore was reading nearby on a large bench. The sisters greeted Salvatore and he took off his hat and hugged them hello each in turn. Bright and articulate well beyond his years, Salvatore was still boyish enough not to be embarrassed to embrace the women. Although with the good fathers Salvatore always tried to act older than his years, when he talked with the nuns of the convent his boundless youthful curiosity took over.

"I'm reading all about garden plants," he offered without being prompted. "Did you know that tomatoes and potatoes are related and that people used to think that tomatoes were poisonous and that when potatoes were first brought to Europe that people thought you were supposed to eat the leaves just like an ordinary vegetable and they all got sick?"

Sister Maria smiled and asked the boy what he knew about tarragon.

"I know it tastes like licorice," Salvatore answered without hesitation, "and that the French use it. The Iranians, too. I think it smells super, though it has been known to cause cancer in mice."

"Really?" asked Sister St. Elizabeth, charmed by Salvatore's patter. "Where did you ever learn such a thing?"

"From Father Balthasar. Well, from the books he has in his library. He has all kinds of books on plants, including some really good ones on different poisonous kinds. He was going to be a farmer once. He told me about it. He lived on a farm and had animals and grew all kinds of vegetables and flowers. Did you know that you can eat almost every kind of animal and you won't die, but if you eat a lot of different plants without knowing what you're doing you could. Vegetarians have to be really careful. That's what Father told me."

The nuns nodded, amused at the flood of words.

Encouraged, Salvatore continued. "And did you know that Socrates, who lived a long time ago and was really smart, ate a plant called hemlock and died? And if you take an elderberry stem and put it in your mouth to use as a blowgun the sap in the stem can kill you?"

"How very strange!" Sister St. Elizabeth said, feigning horror. "But why would anyone need a blowgun?"

"I think it would be fun to have one, but I would never use it. Most plant stems aren't straight and hollow, but elderberry stems are, which makes them great for blowguns."

"And I thought Father Balthasar was just teaching you Latin and how to serve Mass," Sister Maria gently chided.

"Oh, Sister, you know I already know how to serve at Mass. And Latin is also really good for learning plant names, like *Amanita verna*. That means 'spring mushroom' and it's my new favorite! It's a really poisonous mushroom that's white all over and very pretty and looks delicious. Its common name is 'Destroying Angel,' though it's so poisonous that it really should be called Destroying Devil. I've never found one, but it's in all the books."

Sister St. Elizabeth and Sister Maria exchanged uneasy glances as Salvatore prattled on.

"If you eat even a tiny bit of *Amanita verna* you'll never get better. Say, by accident, you take a bite. For a whole day nothing happens. Then it's too late. You get really, really sick—throwing up and other stuff—for hours. And then, just when you wish you were dead, everything seems to go away! You get better... but not really."

Sister St. Elizabeth put her hand over her mouth.

"It's true!" Salvatore's eyes were bright. "Just when you think it's over and you start to feel happy again, the poison attacks your liver and your kidneys and pretty much melts them. There's nothing any doctor in the world can do! You suffer really badly for four, five, six days. You cry all the time, I bet. And then you die."

"Salvatore!" Sister Maria cried, red-faced. "This is not what you should be talking about, nor what we want to hear! Come, let's take a walk around the garden and you can tell us instead about the herbs we grow."

"Okay!" Salvatore said happily, as if one topic were as

good as another. "I already told you about tarragon. Basil tastes a little like it. 'Basil' means 'king.' Which makes sense since it really is the best. It's a kind of mint. Most people don't know that. Fennel tastes like licorice, too. And here's thyme, which I don't really like, and sage and rosemary. They smell a little like the paints Sister Irene uses for her paintings."

"You mean they smell like turpentine?" Sister St. Elizabeth asked.

"Well," Salvatore responded, "like oil paint."

Sister Maria smiled and looked wistfully up at the clear blue sky. "Sister Irene paints the most heavenly portraits of saints, Sister St. Elizabeth. They look right at you, and even when you move, their eyes seem to follow you. But they always have the most peaceful expressions on their faces."

The small group strolled companionably in silence.

Then Salvatore's voice breeched the calm. "Can I ask you something?"

"Of course, my child," Sister Maria replied.

"It's about the boys who come to mow the lawn and prune the trees." His voice was hesitant at first. "They know I'm an orphan. They tease me when no one's around."

A wave of concern passed over the nuns' faces.

"A lot of them are Muslim boys. And they say, well, they say that I look like one of them. That I'm not really Italian, but one of them. They say my parents were probably refugees who didn't want me so they left me at the orphanage."

Sister Maria reached out to touch Salvatore's shoulder.

"There's one really mean boy who says my father was a Syrian or a Turk who raped some Italian girl, and that when

I came out she didn't want me, so she left me with the nuns."

Sister Maria froze, but Salvatore was too deep into his thoughts to notice.

"He says she was 'dishonored' and—and he called my mother a bad name. I don't want to tell you the word." Salvatore paused and looked up into Sister Maria's face. "Do you think it's true?"

"Oh Salvatore!" Sister St. Elizabeth couldn't help from blurting out. "You have the best Italian name and a handsome Italian face, and you are so wonderfully bright. Why else would Father Balthasar have taken on your education himself? Even as a visitor I can see how you are loved. Don't listen to the hurtful words of those mean-spirited boys!"

Salvatore shook his head. "I try not to. I keep telling them that my parents were Italians who died and the nuns took me in, because that's what the nuns always say—but I get the feeling they're not telling the truth." He turned to Sister Maria and whispered, "Do you know where I came from?"

Sister St. Elizabeth looked over at Sister Maria, whose face was as white and whose eyes were as red as any she had ever witnessed in all her years ministering to the poor and rejected. "Thank you for showing me the garden," she said suddenly. "I must go." And then Sister St. Elizabeth did exactly what the nuns of the Convent of St. Paul were commanded by Mother Superior never to do—she left Salvatore alone with his mother.

Sorrow

Sister Maria Fidelis finally found her voice. "I cannot tell you where you came from Salvatore, only that you are surrounded by those who love you. We are your family, and that's what matters. And because of blessed Father Balthasar, who understood from the first how bright and special you are, he and Father Adrian and all of the sisters here are helping you become the best Christian who ever lived! You are not a Muslim. Muslims believe in a false god and we have our Lord Jesus Christ to protect us."

"But, sister," Salvatore interjected, "their god is really, really strong. He can do whatever he wants. Jesus died and their god didn't."

"Oh, Salvatore, let me hold you! How do you know to say such things! Please, let's put upsetting talk aside and walk together, just a little further together, and you can tell me more about the plants in our herb garden."

Still agitated, Salvatore nevertheless did not argue further with Sister Maria. "Okay. Well, we grow parsley and borage, and also many pretty roses," he began.

"Yes, of course!" Maria replied, eager to encourage this

new train of discussion. "We use the parsley all the time, and sometimes we use rose petals for flavoring. We grow borage for medicinal purposes."

"Yes. And do you know that's rue growing over there, against the fence?"

Sister Maria followed the line of Salvatore's outstretched arm. "I see. It's very pretty, isn't it? Grey and not so green."

"Uh-huh," Salvatore agreed. "It gets yellow flowers, but the whole plant is kind of stinky. It tastes terrible, too. Plant it once and it comes up every year. Forever."

"If it tastes terrible, I wonder why we grow it?" Maria mused.

"My book say that nuns grow rue to give to women who have been dishonored—so they can abort their babies."

Maria gasped and backed away from Salvatore. "Why would you say such a terrible thing? Why would you even think it?"

Salvatore's reply was bloodless. "Because I'm happy that my mother didn't eat any rue when I was growing inside of her—but maybe someday she'll be sad that she didn't."

Conversions

Balthasar, Adrian, and Sister Maria alike suffered a solitary unsettled summer that year. In the Vatican, the two priests spent almost all their time apart. They each reflected repeatedly on the revelation Balthasar had made about using the DNA from the Shroud and each knew how seriously it had maimed their friendship. Balthasar often attempted to talk with Adrian, but Adrian simply waved him off.

Adrian couldn't put aside his conviction that Balthasar had done something truly sinful, against God and Maria alike. But in time he also recognized that Balthasar was driven to his sin by a kind of madness, an insanity Adrian did not, and could not, have anticipated. Shouldn't he try to help his old friend rather than curse and reject him? But even if Adrian looked at the priest as a doddering scientist, mad rather than solely prideful, this still left him feeling somehow complicit in a terrible secret.

In the midst of all he now knew, Adrian had one tiny rationalization, one small consolation: It was the knowledge that there wasn't a chance in the rational world that Balthasar's "sacred intervention" had any possibility of having succeeded. Even Balthasar recognized that for what he did to Maria to work, God would need to intervene. And Adrian knew that God wasn't in the habit of intervening on the side of madness. Ultimately, Father Adrian decided it was best to say nothing and keep a watchful eye on Balthasar, for further signs of insanity, and Salvatore, for further signs of trouble.

For her part, Sister Maria had taken to long walks alone to sit and pray the rosary under the magnificent ancient sycamore that shaded the lower end of the Vatican gardens. Well-loved among the convent's residents, not least by Mother Superior, and ever mindful of Salvatore's origins and the trauma she had suffered, Maria was given more leave than the others to work things out in this way, on her own.

Back in the Garden

One sunny early fall afternoon, having finished praying, Maria looked up from her beads to see Salvatore in the distance talking to the young gardeners raking the first fallen leaves. He seemed to be giving them orders before turning away in her direction.

Maria was surprised. These were the same boys Salvatore told her and Sister St. Elizabeth had teased him so unmercifully.

These gardeners were mostly Rome's Muslim youth the Vatican officials, in their infinite wisdom, thought would be good to employ, to help support their families and show them that Catholicism was not their enemy but their partner.

When Salvatore noticed Maria, he ran up and hugged her.

Maria stifled a flinch, then sighed and held him tight. "I thought those boys teased you, Salvatore. It looks like you've made peace."

Salvatore pulled away and puffed out his chest. "Oh, they don't tease me anymore. In fact, sometimes I bully them now—but only a little."

Maria stiffened. "Oh, dear! You mustn't bully, Salvatore.

Not anyone, not even a little."

"Well, I learned some new stuff I read in two books. One on when Jesus was a baby and growing up, and the other in a book Father Adrian let me look at one time." Salvatore grinned. "You can learn *everything* from books!"

"What was the book that talked about the child Jesus?" Sister Maria asked.

"It's called 'The Apocryphal Gospels.'"

"What? Where in the world did you get that book?"

"You know Father Balthasar lets me study in his library. I found it on the top shelf. It's amazing! It has all these wonderful stories in it. There's one where a boy accidently bumped into Jesus and Jesus made him die. And when the boy's parents went to Joseph to complain, Jesus made them all blind! Another time, when someone let the water out of a pool that Jesus was playing with, Jesus shriveled him up and he died, too—"

"Stop!" Sister Maria cried. "Those are not holy stories! Not one of them is true."

"Oh, no, Sister, I know they're true. The Apostle Thomas wrote them down and lots of people believe them. I believe them, too. Our Lord Jesus was teaching us not to be bullied—by anyone! Thomas wrote that one day, when Joseph was mad at Jesus and pulled him by the ear, Jesus told him, 'Don't make me angry and never touch me like that again!' Then Joseph told Mary not to let their son out of the house since everyone who annoyed or made Jesus angry died." Salvatore's eyes flashed as he spoke. "And besides, everyone says bullying is a sin, and Jesus is just telling us to do all we can to make it stop!"

There was a pause as Maria gathered courage to ask. "Salvatore, did you say to those boys that bullying is a sin, and they stopped? Or are you going to—"

Salvatore laughed. "I wish! But I don't have magic powers like Jesus did. But I did do something."

Hesitant, Maria asked, "What did you do?"

"It's something I read about in a book on self-defense that Father Adrian showed me. He used to be a boxer, you know. The book said that you can stop even a grown man by punching him in the front of his neck, on his Adam's apple. You can even kill him if you do it hard enough."

Maria's terrified face only encouraged Salvatore to continue. "It's true! So the next time Ali—remember, he's the older boy who called my mother a bad word—said it again I just walked right up to him and punched him in the Adam's apple. In front of everybody! He fell down and started to choke and cry."

Maria gasped.

"Don't worry, Sister. He didn't die. My punch made him say he was sorry. So we became friends, I guess. And I was happy about it, for a little while, but then he started teasing me again. About how I'm not really Italian. In fact, he said that there's a man in Rome—I think he's a bad man—and that I look just like him. Ali said he's going to bring him someday soon to work on the garden crew, so I can meet my real father and I won't be a worthless orphan anymore. And I said—"

With a wail Sister Maria turned and fled back to the convent, leaving Salvatore alone, and finally speechless, in the garden.

CLASH

That Those with Eyes May See

I t was only when the first signs of autumn appeared that Adrian was finally able to communicate with Balthasar again without recoiling. He used the opportunity of mentioning the popular upcoming annual fair held by the sisters of the Convent of St. Paul to Balthasar as a gesture of good will toward the old priest. Life presses forward, and Adrian had accepted his own decision to remain silent, but watchful.

One Friday in mid-autumn, all the sisters minus one had gathered for Mass at dawn. Sister Irene, the artist among them, had kept to her bed because of throbbing pains in her head and neck.

Sister Irene was one of the older nuns in the convent. Despite a certain kindness hidden in her face, she was, candidly and by all accounts, a plain, almost homely, woman. But nothing like this was apparent in her portraits of saints and martyrs. Whether male or female, young or old, they were each handsome and lovely, sparkling in their inner happiness, and radiant in the joy that comes from holiness.

Irene had exhausted herself completing the series of small portraits she had been working on all year to put on sale at the fair, which the sisters would hold that day. As she lay in bed she was grateful she had managed to take her work downstairs the evening before and set it up in a quiet, sheltered spot just outside the convent, and near to her window.

How her head ached! Despite her fatigue it was hard to rest. She heard the chapel bell ring and tried to follow in her mind the order of the Mass she was missing. Then she heard a noise. *At this hour? It must be the gardeners*, she thought. But something made her drag herself out of bed and over to the window to check.

In the dawning light she could see three adolescent boys gathered by her paintings. They were doing something to them. She threw open the window with a cry. "*Stop!* Leave my paintings alone!"

The youths ran off.

Shaken, head throbbing even more fiercely, Sister Irene dressed and rushed outside.

The eyes of every saint and martyr had been gouged out of her paintings.

The nuns returned from Mass to find Sister Irene hysterical, surrounded by her blinded portraits.

Mother Superior ran for the priests. "Please—can you come and give something to calm Sister Irene?"

"What happened?" asked Father Balthasar.

"All her paintings have been destroyed!" cried Mother

Superior. "The eyes are gone on every one. They stare out blankly. It's horrible."

"Who would do such a thing?" Father Adrian wondered.

"She said she thought the gardeners did it—the young gardeners."

"Now why would they do that to Sister Irene?" asked Father Balthasar.

"I don't think it's personal, Father," Adrian interjected. "I doubt that they have anything against Irene. No, it's far more ideological."

Father Balthasar and Mother Superior exchanged uneasy glances.

"Some iconoclasts in Byzantium gouged out the eyes of icons they considered idolatrous," Adrian explained. "And when they could get away with it, the more puritan Protestants defaced the art in Catholic and Anglican churches. In fact, Muslims throughout the world, though mostly in Turkey and Greece, have been committing such acts and worse for centuries."

Suddenly Adrian remembered something—something he decided not to mention. The last time he had such a discussion about fanatics and their unholy relationship to eyes was with Salvatore, during their study of the early conquest of the Mediterranean by Muslims. Yes, Salvatore had definitely seemed fascinated—but, no, he couldn't be involved in the destruction of Sister Irene's paintings, because Salvatore had been with Adrian and Balthasar this morning, serving Mass.

Omar Sadiq

T hree or four times a year Balthasar called his friend Omar Sadiq, head of one of Rome's many mosques. Advent had ended, Christmas had come and was just now gone, and the new year would be here soon. Since they were overdue to chat, Balthasar decided to invite Omar for a cup of nonalcoholic post-holiday cheer.

Omar's mosque was a just few blocks from the western edge of the Vatican, across the main *viale*, not far from the towers of the old Radio Vaticana inside the gardens. Father Balthasar knew Omar from their attendance at all of those interfaith dialogue conferences that religious and semi-religious activists were forever putting together. (These were the kinds of events that caused in Father Adrian an almost tangible revulsion. He managed to avoid them with supreme regularity.) In any event, Balthasar and Omar were acquaintances and then friends for quite a while before Balthasar brought Omar into the Vatican to introduce him to Adrian.

Physically, the Imam Omar, as he was known throughout the city, was short and stout, with an olive complexion. Behind sorrowful brown eyes, he had the look of one always thinking. And if he gave the impression of otherworldly distraction it was because he did not inhabit this moment, but lived in the next—thinking, imagining, wondering.

Omar was a Sunni Muslim, as were almost all the Muslims of his generation in Rome, before the latest migrations. Originally from Lebanon, he spoke Italian with a Middle Eastern voice as well as a pleasing French lilt. Indeed, the one disagreement Balthasar had with Omar was that Omar always wanted to speak Italian or English to Father, and Balthasar always wanted to improve his passably adequate Arabic with Omar.

A widower, the Imam was raising two sons alone, one a teenager and the other just twelve. Omar was also the most courageous man in all of Rome. While so many other imams counseled suspicion, Omar counseled trust. Where others argued for jihad, Omar preached peace. He believed in peace with all his heart. "*Salam*," he would say, "is just like '*Shalom*'—peace." And "*Salam*" and "Islam" were really one and the same: "Islam is Peace."

The sermons he preached every Friday were more or less the same: "Allah has called all of us in this congregation, and each of us personally, to pray, to give alms, and to be at peace with our neighbors." He even recently told his listeners that the parable in Luke of the Good Samaritan, who out of charity helped his religious antagonist when he was hurt and in distress, was not just a story told by Jesus, "it is the word of Allah as well." This cost Omar a number of followers, and speaking in their own mosques the following Friday two other imams actually called Imam Omar an apostate. But Omar said only what he believed.

To his detractors, Omar's sermons were never strict enough, never orthodox enough, although in reality he spoke about more than love and peace and respecting other faiths. He was a scholar after all—a scholar of the Koran, of the history of Islam and the teachings of the Prophet. But everyone knew, or came to see, that his teachings, his interpretations of the faith, were more akin to a classroom discussion or a secular philosophy seminar. In contrast to the fiery, pointed, and intense sermons of so many of his fellow imams, Omar often began speaking in this vein: "Now what exactly do we think the words we have just heard might mean? For Allah certainly cannot intend for us to despise others whom He has also created or to slaughter people in His name. We all know that that cannot be."

His sermons gained such notoriety that Omar became the darling of the ecumenical community and the preferred speaker for every multifaith gathering. Yet nothing rises without something falling. The year earlier, Rome's Council of Muslim Scholars issued a warning to Omar, and by the following year a small majority of Sunni clerics moved to declare his teachings heretical. Though he had a respectful but never large following of other liberal Sunni imams, over the years Omar found himself speaking to a congregation in his own mosque that grew smaller and more unsettled every Friday. Then Omar began to receive death threats, every one beginning with the same words: "In the name of Allah, the Most Gracious and Merciful…"

Undeterred, Imam Omar continued to preach his sermons of peace, toleration, and mutual respect.

Omar the Collaborator

Many years ago the good imam's mosque had been among the largest in Rome. But now, despite the influx of tens of thousands of Muslims from Somalia and Egypt and Tunisia and more recently Libya and Syria, his congregation was dwindling. What was once one of the most important, respected houses of Islamic instruction in Rome had become, at least within the Muslim community, something of a backwater—and what was worse, a problem.

The latest surge of migrants brought with it the young and more clearly fanatical element, who whispered "Christian collaborator" at the mention of Imam Omar's name. And as the city's Muslim community became increasingly radicalized, Omar became, perhaps paradoxically, more outspokenly moderate. But while this moderation endeared the imam to the general religious community of Rome, it only made him increasingly suspect among the growing devout Muslim fold.

"You're pretty much the only Muslim I trust," Father Adrian admitted to Omar not long after they first met, when Adrian surprised himself by confiding in Omar his visceral dislike of Islam. He explained that in growing up among Muslims in his parents' working-class neighborhood west of London, he had learned by listening and experience to perceive them as little more than clannish, thieving criminals. It was a meeting of minds as well as spirit, for Omar, to Adrian's shock, thought pretty much the same thing.

Still, there was a time, centuries ago, Omar always insisted, when Islam defined the pinnacle of civilization. Back when Adrian's ancestors were living in cold stone huts hoping to kill a rabbit or even a rat to stay alive, Omar's family was eating pastries with honey and apricots and pistachios, preserving the writings of the great Greek philosophers from destruction, advancing medical science, astronomy, mathematics and, above all, building mosques of intricate beauty and writing the finest poetry imaginable.

"Then something happened," Omar sighed. "The Muslim world began to reject science just as the West began to discover it. In the West, every scientific advance bred a thousand new discoveries, and these discoveries, as you know, meant power. As the Muslim world regressed, sinking deeper into anti-scientific ignorance, the West unlocked all the secrets of Nature, and would soon rule the world."

"Yes," added Father Adrian. "It wasn't exactly power or force that made the Christian countries great—it was knowledge."

Omar nodded and continued. "Yes, but knowledge empowered them to do whatever they wished. The West explored the world. It took for itself gold and spices and foods. It built cathedrals in little cities that put the great mosques of the East to shame. It invented the press, and soon literacy and science and philosophy spread. Its music was lovelier than the music the angels played. The Christian West remade culture and redefined civilization, and it invented the armaments to defend it and preserve what it had created forever. As Europe rose, Islam sank."

Omar's eyes grew sadder whenever he mused upon this history. He catalogued in his head every year of Islam's decline. And yet, unlike most Muslims, who felt cheated and humiliated by Christendom's rise and Islam's fall, Omar argued that "there is no barrier to Islam following in the footsteps of the West. Islam had science back when the West had only superstition. We could have science again."

Balthasar the scientist, and party to many of these discussions, nodded in agreement.

Omar was speaking now with more energy. "Islam had great art. We can have great art again. And Islam can be rich again. All we need to understand is one word: freedom."

Father Adrian broke in, "Freedom to inquire, freedom to think, freedom to make, discover, learn, do—it's been that freedom that has made the West all that it is."

"Sadly, freedom has become anathema to Islam," Omar countered, his voice trailing away. Although he always said "Islam is peace," he knew more fundamentally that Islam meant "submission." And submission is the very opposite of freedom.

"The slaves and servants of Allah," was how his fellow Muslims described themselves. But slaves are not free, and servants do little on their own. So Omar devoted his life not to rejecting Islam and the Koran—that would do nothing to raise up the community—but rather to showing how the Koran could be seen as encouraging inquiry, toleration, and initiative. To how the Koran stood not for submission, but for *liberty*.

This is why Balthasar and Omar got on so well. This aspect of modernity was central to both their outlooks. But Adrian and Omar became even closer insofar as both men *felt* the same way: that the everyday Muslim world was unendingly problematic. After one particularly thorny discussion that left them more than a little exhausted, Omar reminded Adrian of Churchill's famous words:

How dreadful are the curses which Mohammedanism lays on its votaries! Besides the fanatical frenzy, which is as dangerous in a man as hydrophobia in a dog, there is this fearful fatalistic apathy. The effects are apparent in many countries—improvident habits, slovenly systems of agriculture, sluggish methods of commerce, and insecurity of property exist wherever the followers of the Prophet rule or live. A degraded sensualism deprives this life of its grace and refinement, the next of its dignity and sanctity. The fact that in Mohammedan law every woman must belong to some man as his absolute property, either as a child, a wife, or a concubine, must delay the final extinction of slavery until the faith of Islam has ceased to be a great power among men. Individual Moslems may show splendid qualities, but the influence of the religion paralyses the social development of those who follow it. No stronger retrograde force exists in the world. Far from being moribund, Mohammedanism is a militant and proselytizing faith. It has already spread throughout Central Africa, raising fearless warriors at every step; and were it not that Christianity is sheltered in the strong arms of science, the science against which it had vainly struggled, the civilization of modern Europe might fall, as fell the civilization of ancient Rome.

On Churchill's fierce criticisms, Omar and Adrian agreed. But while Omar believed that Islam could be saved from all this, Adrian doubted that it ever could—and still be Islam.

Secrets

As Salvatore approached his teenage years, Balthasar would sit in his study reviewing the young man's spiritual and educational development. Although Balthasar and Adrian had eventually "reconciled," Balthasar's confession and Adrian's response always hovered between them. And while it never ceased to unsettle him, Balthasar had long grown accustomed to a certain judging watchfulness in Adrian that appeared whenever Salvatore was present. But as time passed and the more they both witnessed the boy's incredible development, facilitated by their careful tutelage, the more Balthasar returned to his former certainty that God had led him to act rightly.

Salvatore continued to be a prodigy in all his studies. His facility with every language set before him—Latin, Greek, and English, then Hebrew and Arabic—now seemed complete. Balthasar and Adrian continued teaching Salvatore mathematics. They began him on Euclid when he was no more than five, then in time took him through Descartes and Newton all the way to Boole, Leibniz, and Lobachevsky. And while Salvatore understood the language of mathematics, and had an easy facility with its concepts and applications, he treated it more as a game to be played rather than as the serious language of Nature. To Adrian's occasional frustration, Salvatore never seemed to give it much heed.

The same was true for science. Balthasar taught the young Salvatore all the landmarks, from every experiment from Archimedes through problems in relativity and topics in atomic theory. But Salvatore, while he understood it all, had little interest in the field. "He certainly doesn't have your devotion science and technology," Adrian pointed out from time to time.

It was in philosophy where Salvatore shone. Logic, metaphysics, epistemology. Aristotle, Aquinas, Kant, Maritain. He mastered ideas and could weigh, compare, and discourse on them more naturally than so many of the wisest Jesuits teaching at the Pontifical Gregorian University in downtown Rome.

Yet even more than in philosophy, Salvatore shone brightest in theology. At an unnervingly young age, he seemed to have mastered the biblical text, both Old and New Testaments, with a scholar's mind and a believer's passion. Although he shied away from putting this suspicion to the test, Balthasar thought Salvatore probably had the whole of Scripture committed to memory, every line, every word. "Truly," Balthasar thought with a mix of smugness and awe, "truly this is the Son of God."

And yet a few things still troubled the old priest and teacher's conviction. For a long time he'd tried to interest Salvatore in the religions of the East, in Hindu mysticism, and in the various Confucian and Buddhist writings. But while Balthasar loved to mull over such mysterious spirituality, Salvatore would have none of it. And Balthasar was concerned that Salvatore was not only uninterested, but that he held these venerable texts and traditions in contempt.

Balthasar thought a good heart could find something of value in almost any religion, but Salvatore never had the same sensibility. The Hebrew Scriptures, the New Testament, even the Koran and the various sayings and histories of Muhammad, Salvatore devoured. "All things connected with the Book," he explained to Balthasar, "are instructive and conducive to life everlasting." But he had no qualms declaring all other religious texts and traditions "useless distractions," and that knowing anything about them was "pedantry and intellectual vanity."

The old priest was stunned, but despite the fact that Salvatore had a few sharper edges than Balthasar expected, or felt comfortable with, despite the fact that he seemed less tolerant and open than Balthasar would have anticipated, it was clear that Salvatore had a facility with concepts and ideas, a genius for getting to the core of an issue, and a power of speech that no other adolescent had or, Balthasar imagined, ever had.

It was obvious that the time was at hand when Balthasar's "student" would become his teacher. On one level, this was the most exhilarating possibility imaginable. Balthasar hungered for nothing more in this life than *to know*: to gain the secrets of the universe, to understand the ground of all morality, to unlock the human heart, to plunge into the depths of the Divine Nature, to see the interconnections of all of God's creation, to catch a deeper glimpse of the unity of the Cosmos.

And to sit at the knee of the revivified Son of God—*to learn all truth from the Word Himself*—the very promise of it electrified Balthasar. Like the disciples conversing with Christ on the road to Emmaus, all the scales would be lifted from his eyes, and he would soon see everything clearly.

Still, despite his longing for these things, in those moments when Balthasar allowed himself to dwell on such thoughts—something nagged at him. What was it that always seemed to gnaw away bits of his anticipated joy?

"Do I fear being proven wrong on some important topic?" he asked himself in the quiet of a sleepless night, which were occurring with greater frequency lately. "Could it be hubris?" Balthasar wondered, pacing his room. "Could it be pride in not wanting to be replaced by my student, even when he is the Savior?" Or was it some even darker worry? Balthasar paused, his face covered in midnight shadow. For all his learning and erudition, he could not give these secret misgivings a name.

Day Darkens

On the Second Sunday of Advent, December 2025, Balthasar's nagging doubts suddenly deepened. Mass began with the words of Isaiah, "People of Zion, behold the Lord shall come for the salvation of all nations." This gave Balthasar the opportunity to talk in his brief homily about a frequent theme: God's love for the Jews as His people and how He built upon them to bring salvation to everyone. "We Christians owe the Jews our love and respect," Balthasar explained to his congregants, "not only because they are deserving as our equals as fellow human beings, but in a special way, because it was through the Jewish people that God saved the world—saved each and every one of us."

As was their custom, after Mass the priest changed from his liturgical vestments, his acolyte put aside his tunic, and, dressed in their regular clothes, Balthasar and Salvatore would sit down to talk about the readings and the homily. Salvatore seemed to learn more from these interactive discussions than he did from listening to Mass, and he always wore the bright perkiness of the teacher's best student.

On this morning, however, Salvatore looked puzzled, almost weary. "Why do you praise the Jews so much, Father?"

"As I said during my homily, in a special way salvation came to us through them. If it weren't for the Jewish race we—"

"No," Salvatore interrupted, "wasn't it *despite* the Jews that salvation came into the world? It wasn't as if they opened the door for our Lord and Savior. They fought Him, they contradicted Him, they betrayed Him to Pilate. They demanded His death."

Balthasar was unnerved by the quiet severity in Salvatore's voice.

"Remember, Father, it was Paul who renounced his Jewish name and his Jewish faith. Paul brought the Word to Rome and to the Greeks—to the whole world. Paul even had to fight the more 'Jewish' apostles, like James and even Peter, our first pope, to spread God's word everywhere."

Always polite and respectful during their discussions, this was the first time Salvatore had ever openly contradicted anything Father had to say. Balthasar took a deep breath and reiterated, almost verbatim, the points he made in his homily, then added, "The great truth is that the Jews have now suffered for two thousand years for what was done. More than sufficient expiation has been paid. Any sin has by now been forgiven."

Salvatore looked doubtful.

"Surely the Jews have suffered enough," Balthasar repeated gently.

Salvatore leaned forward and looked directly at Balthasar. "Suffered enough? Who are we to know God's mind so well as to tell Him what is *enough*? Maybe when a people rejects God and tries to kill His Messenger it is never 'enough.'" The boy's voice was low and came close to trembling with an anger Balthasar had never witnessed. Then, just as abruptly, Salvatore collected himself. He knelt before the old priest, requested his blessing, and asked to be excused.

Father Balthasar watched the boy rush away with a sinking heart. He tried to tell himself that it wasn't that serious, that Salvatore was just pushing back a little—after all, he was on the brink of turning sixteen years old—pushing back in order to get greater clarity of the truth. That, at least, was what Balthasar wrote in his diary later that day, but his hand kept shaking.

A Distant Dawn

This act of independence on Salvatore's part forced Father Balthasar to consider how someday, someday very soon, he would have to explain to Salvatore exactly who Balthasar believed Salvatore to be—his divine origin, how he wasn't a foundling, how the sainted Sister Maria Fidelis was actually his earthly mother, and above all, how he, Balthasar, had brought Christ-as-Salvatore to life through his art.

Balthasar recognized that he has been hoping all along he wouldn't have to do this. That he was hoping, ardently, that his Divinity would gradually appear on its own to Salvatore. That Salvatore would grow into self-knowledge as people say that Christ grew in a fuller understanding of Himself over time.

But though he was surely growing in wisdom and age, Balthasar had to acknowledge that Salvatore seemed not to have the slightest glimmer of who he actually was. "Give it another half-year," Balthasar often argued with himself. "Better yet, give it another year. Then, if Salvatore still seems unaware, I will tell him."

"How contradictory that sounds," he mused one day. "If

nothing changes within the next year, it will be my divine obligation to bring the full truth to Salvatore—to enlighten, in a sense, the Divine Light itself."

The Lessons of History

Despite his own misgivings about Salvatore's origins, after Balthasar's confession Father Adrian continued to put his all into the young man's education. Lately, literature and history had become their central subjects, and Salvatore enjoyed them both. This was especially true when it came to Western civilization. To Salvatore, it was a grand parade of crazy kings and queens, wild battles, and rise and fall of empires. Even though Adrian approached this history systematically and chronologically—the Fall of Rome, the coming Dark Ages, the rise of the Church and the Papacy, the Crusades, the Renaissance followed by the Reformation, and with it the great war between Catholics and Protestants—he moved through the centuries with a passionate intensity that belied his otherwise staid, sometimes almost chilly, demeanor.

Adrian presented this grand history as he saw it, through the lens of the Church and through the prism of the great theological debates—Arianism, Nestorianism, the split between Catholicism and the Orthodox Church and its consequences, the errors of Luther, the madness and brutality of Calvin and his followers—and yet, while Salvatore's interest in the nuances of theology and theological debate was genuine, he showed far more vigorous interest in history's battles.

For example, Salvatore had memorized every movement of the crusaders over the long history of the many Crusades. On his own he had reconstructed a model of Jerusalem and with it models of all the forces and siege instruments to breach the sacred city's walls in 1099. He could recount every battle's most gruesome episodes with relish, the more brutal the better. To Adrian this was representative of somewhat standard boyish attraction to blood and mayhem, and easy proof that Salvatore could not be who Balthasar claimed him to be.

When they began a study of Protestant Reformation in England, Adrian decided to make the lesson personal. "Staunch Catholics throughout the Reformation, my family was almost destroyed because they would never swear allegiance to the English Church," Adrian recounted to Salvatore. "Generations of my ancestors were hanged, and many tortured, for their allegiance to Rome. In fact, my namesake, my Great-Great-Great-and so on Uncle Adrian even suffered all the horrors of bloody martyrdom."

Salvatore seemed riveted by this, so Adrian expounded.

"You see, Uncle Adrian had gone to France and then to Rome, where he became a Jesuit priest. This was during the last few years of Queen Elizabeth's rule. Adrian returned England to minister to his family and to the rough and poor country souls who tried to cling to the Faith throughout the years of the great prosecution. Once this was discovered, Adrian was tortured daily for weeks. But despite all the torments, Adrian never broke. He was eventually dragged to the gallows and hanged—and more."

Salvatore didn't move a muscle.

"Here are the words that were read to my ancestor, Father Adrian, when convicted of being a Jesuit traitor to his queen:

You shall be taken from your cell back to the place where you were found, and from thence be drawn on a hurdle to the place of execution, where you shall be hanged by the neck, but not till you are dead. Then you shall be taken down while yet alive, and your bowels shall be cut out from your body and burnt before your face. While yet alive, if you are so spared, your bowels will be eaten by dogs, again before your face. Then your head shall be cut off, to be at the Queen's disposal, and your body cut in four quarters. And may God Almighty have mercy on your soul."

Adrian's words were met by silence. Although Salvatore was clearly captivated by the tale, the shock, horror, sadness Adrian expected never came. "What did the queen do with Adrian's head?" Salvatore asked instead, his eyes glistening. "Did she keep it? Did the dogs really eat his guts?"

Adrian couldn't bring himself to respond.

Without changing his expression Salvatore made an observation, seemingly to himself. "*Wow*. People took God seriously back then. Too bad we don't see things that way now."

Adrian flinched. "No, Salvatore, it's good we don't see

things that way anymore. I'm as firm a believer in our Faith as you will find anywhere, but I don't believe we should murder people who hold a different belief."

"Really?" Salvatore retorted. "Even if God wants you to? Even if God *commands* you?"

"God would never command a person to do evil—not ever, Salvatore."

"But He could, Father. He could if He wanted to."

Adrian could not believe the turn the conversation had taken. "Why in the world would God ever want you to do evil?"

The boy answered too quickly. "Maybe to teach us that evil is what He says is evil, just like good is whatever He says is good. It's not people who make things good or bad— only God. Didn't God tell Abraham to kill Isaac? We say that killing is evil, Father, but God told Abraham to kill his very own son!"

"But God stopped him, Salvatore."

"Yes—but not until *after* Abraham was going to do it. And after God stopped Abraham, God praised Abraham for agreeing to kill his own son. God blessed him and promised him great rewards for agreeing to do what you say is evil, and all because Abraham said yes to the voice of God without hesitation or question."

A Bitter Glass

H is mind ringing with Salvatore's zealous words about evil, God's will, and rewarding Abraham, Father Adrian went straight to Balthasar's door and knocked.

"Adrian!" Balthasar looked surprised and relieved to see him. He dared a welcoming smile. "Please... do come in."

Adrian waved away the offer. "Forgive me, Balthasar, for being more candid than I think you want me to be."

Balthasar's smile faded. "Adrian, you know I'll always forgive you. Please, what is it?"

"Salvatore is strange, Balthasar. I know what you think he is, but I don't mean different or special—or unique." Adrian watched Balthasar put his hand to his heart, and plunged ahead. "There's something truly uncivilized about him. Why would your supposed Reincarnation relish tales of torture and suffering and death? Why would your new Christ argue that evil is sometimes acceptable?" Adrian watched his old friend's face turn white. "This isn't the Christ I know. This person isn't the Christ of the Gospels."

Balthasar stared into Adrian's eyes for a long, tortured moment before responding. "If Christ thought as we do, he wouldn't be Christ; he'd be a creature of our own making. Consider all those poor souls who say they worship a transcendent God when all they worship are their own ideas, which they ascribe to God."

"This isn't the time for a sermon," Adrian retorted.

But Balthasar continued. "If your God agrees with you on all the issues of the day you can rest assured that you made him up. Remember what the Scriptures say: 'God's ways are not our ways.'"

"That's the easy answer, Balthasar, and you know it!"

"You want the hard answer?" Balthasar glared at Adrian, and then something inside him seemed to falter. "The more complete answer is... I don't know." Balthasar put his face in his hands, which troubled Adrian even more than what the old priest acknowledged next. "I've seen it, you've seen it, even the sisters whisper about it."

"Yes," Father Adrian agreed. "The other day Sister Miriam confessed to me that Salvatore seems to have as little of the love Christ as she has ever seen, and I agree. Christ tells us to be just, but merciful; strong, but giving; lovers of life, but willing at any second to give it up. Salvatore sees only half of those paradoxes, Balthasar. He fixates on the darkest parts of the Word of God."

Balthasar nodded reluctantly. "And yet, through all of his ferocity and passion, he seems happy. Not serene—God knows not serene—but somehow happy."

"Even sadists smile," Adrian fired back.

"Adrian!"

The priest could not stop himself. "Tell me something, Balthasar. When you and God have your talks, what does He tell you to do about Salvatore?"

Balthasar's chin hardened.

"Well? He told you what to do with the Shroud. What has He told you to do since then?"

Adrian watched Balthasar's face crumble.

Without another word Adrian crossed the threshold and pulled two glasses from Balthasar's cabinet. For the first time in a long time, the two priests shared a glass of port.

Consider the Lilies

One morning, about three months after he had confronted Father Balthasar about the Jews, Salvatore encountered Sister Teresa of the Child Jesus in the cloister. Sister Teresa had joined the order of Augustinian nuns almost seventy years earlier when she was simply a girl, and she had remained simple in personal habit and in nature throughout her life. Now in her late eighties, she walked with a cane, a joyful half-smile on her lips, her rosary chattering softly at her side.

All of Sister Teresa's questions—never very complicated ones—had been answered years ago. She was here on Earth to pray, to serve as best she could, and to accept what few small sufferings God might send her way to make the future joys of Heaven even sweeter.

Already in her seventies when Salvatore arrived, Sister Teresa had helped midwife the secret birth in what she remembered as an easy delivery, though the circumstances of the conception were difficult to put aside. She remembered holding and kissing poor Maria's hand, pressing a cool cloth to her sister's forehead, and reciting in a soothing voice all the prayers to the Virgin Mary that she knew.

Sister Teresa was in awe of Father Balthasar, who always preached the nicest and mercifully never very long homilies, and she admired Father Adrian, too, even though he was much more no-nonsense. He was never curt with her, really, just more direct. In any event, she actually talked more regularly with Father Adrian, who was her personal confessor, since she hated to bother someone as pensive and wise as Balthasar with her small problems and even smaller observations.

"Salvatore," Sister Teresa exclaimed the morning of their encounter, "you are growing up so strong and smart! Perhaps you will become a doctor or a great scientist. Medicine has come so very far, but it still hasn't been able to cure my arthritis. Maybe you can find a cure and make so many people happy. God would love you for that, and all us old people would bless you. A doctor, yes, a scientific doctor, just like our Father Balthasar."

The old nun did not notice that Salvatore was not smiling. "Ah, Sister Teresa, accept your pain and offer it up to God for the forgiveness of your sins, so that when the Day of Judgment comes He'll not be harsh with you."

"Oh, I hope He won't be harsh with me, Salvatore. I love Him so much. But you'll continue to pray for me, nonetheless, won't you?"

"Do you know why God accepted Abel's offerings but not Cain's?" Salvatore asked.

Sister Teresa was taken aback. She wasn't used to being asked her opinion on theological matters. She thought about it as best she could, but could only respond that God accepted Abel's offering "because Abel must have loved

God more."

"Perhaps you are right, Sister," Salvatore replied, "But it's also clear that God loved *him* more. Why do you think God loved Abel more than he loved Cain?"

Tongue-tied, Sister could only stare at Salvatore, so he answered his own question. "God loved Abel more because Abel was simple. Abel was humble. He 'followed the flock,' the Bible says. He didn't try to change God's creation, or manipulate it for his benefit. He just obeyed. And God shepherded Abel. But Cain, the evil one, pretended to change God's creation, to make it better for himself. He 'cultivated the fields,' the Bible tells us. He didn't pick things where they grew, he planted them. He watered them. He fertilized them and weeded them and pruned them. He made tools and dug down deep into the substance of the earth. He took God's creation and twisted it for his own benefit.

"He did not live like the lilies of the field, Sister. No, he tried to grow lilies and barley and everything after his own fancy. He tried to make his life longer and more comfortable. Although the Bible tells us he was a farmer, it shows us a picture of the true Cain. He was the first scientist. And God rejected the offerings of Cain's science.

"We are called, Sister, to take whatever God sends our way. Why should we seek to put ourselves and our petty desires above God? A doctor? A scientist? That's the surest road to Hell."

What an odd sermon to be preaching, thought Sister Teresa, who was only trying to encourage the boy. Still, simple as she was, she knew enough to say, "You mustn't talk that way, Salvatore! Father Balthasar is as close to God as anyone in this world, and he's the best doctor and scientist in Italy. For all the good he does, for all the good he has done for you, you act as if God will send him to Hell when he's called. Surely you don't mean that. I know you cannot mean that."

"Perhaps I do, Sister," Salvatore said lightly. And with a smile and bow, he turned and strode away.

Celebrating Death

Sister Teresa died just a few weeks after her conversation with Salvatore. He declined to serve as an acolyte for the funeral Mass, although he sat in the chapel and listened intently to the liturgy and to everything Father Balthasar had to say.

Balthasar had been her doctor through Sister Teresa's last days in the infirmary. He did his best to relieve her pain, but, more often than not, she resisted his efforts. She had turned herself over to the Lord, offering up all the suffering that came her way. After all, hers was nothing like Jesus's agony, and he redeemed the whole world through his pain. Maybe she, with her little cup of pain, could help ransom a few poor souls from Purgatory; maybe God would make her joy even brighter if she accepted her suffering as His gift. For she was promised that it would never be more than she could bear, and the promise was surely true.

Now it was Sister Maria's turn to hold the moist towel to Sister Teresa's brow and quietly say all the Marian prayers she knew so that Sister could hear and follow in her mind.

Sister Teresa spoke very little during her last three days, though just before receiving the Holy Eucharist for the final time, she motioned weakly to Balthasar. He leaned forward. "Ask Salvatore to pray for me every day," she whispered in the priest's ear. "I promise to pray for him. I believe he needs it."

Balthasar nodded, but he was unsettled by this unexpected request.

Soon sister's body became progressively colder, from her feet up through her legs, then all over. She died as quietly, as humbly, as she had lived. It was, as we are no longer wont to say, a Happy Death.

Despite Sister Teresa's joy at her coming reunion with the Lord, the sisters of the Convent of St. Paul wept freely at her funeral Mass. Father Balthasar's brief homily was a record of all the simple kindnesses people had received from Sister Teresa throughout her long life. He closed with these words: "We are thankful dear Teresa was with us for so many years and we commemorate her life here today. Let us not dwell on her passing, but remember with grateful hearts the joy she brought into our own lives. By the act of how she lived, Teresa proved that life is a wonderful gift, and that a life of service to others is the most wonderful gift of all."

After the interment in the convent cemetery Balthasar shook the hands of the many in attendance, blessing them as they walked away, whether wiping sad tears or smiling at a happy memory. Salvatore was not among them.

Nor did Salvatore appear as scheduled the next morning to serve at early Mass. In fact, Balthasar did not see Salvatore again until the following Sunday, and then not as an acolyte but as a wooden face in the congregation.

Balthasar had wanted to reach out to Salvatore during the week, but considered that the boy had been more affected by the old nun's death than he expected. *Yes, I think it's best to give Salvatore some time and space to grieve*, he decided. Balthasar simply didn't allow himself to dwell on what Sister's Teresa's deathbed request might imply.

After Mass, it was Salvatore who followed Balthasar into the sacristy. His expression was confrontational.

"Salvatore, please come in. You seem upset. Is something wrong? I haven't seen you since Sister Teresa's funeral."

"Yes, Father, ever since then."

Balthasar quelled a sudden wave of nerves. "I expect her passing affected you deeply—as it did everyone at the convent—but I didn't know you two were so close."

"We weren't 'close,' Father, and she didn't 'pass.' She died. She suffered and then she died. And you made light of it in your homily."

Balthasar was stunned. "I made light of Teresa's death? Why would you say that?"

"Because instead of instructing all those simple nuns sobbing in the pews on the sovereign greatness of death, you fed them a meek and timid story about the sweetness of life. Your words put earthly life over death at a time when death showed its mastery over all the living."

Salvatore began pacing across the room. "*Look at the sweetness of death*, you should have said! Do you sisters not see that Death is God's way of holding humanity close to Him? Without death, we would live only for ourselves. We would forget God. When God chased Adam and Eve out of the garden he gave them suffering as a penance, but he gave them death as a blessing! Only through death can we return to God and be with him forever.

"This is what all martyrs know—that death is necessary before happiness is possible. Christian martyrs once knew this and all of them, you say, are now before the throne of God. But today it seems as if only our Muslim brothers understand this truth. And they die with joy, and God accepts their blood and brings them all to Paradise."

Salvatore paused to face Balthasar.

"You told everyone at the funeral that we should celebrate Teresa's life. Can't you see you've made life into a cult?" Salvatore shook his head in disgust. "You and your tribe can think of nothing higher. Celebrate life? I tell you that you should rather celebrate Death."

Balthasar recoiled. "Salvatore, my son, listen to yourself! You have turned everything backward. No Christian denies that our body must die before we can enter our eternal life. But to lust for death as some fanatics do is a sickness. Those you mention not only love death, they love to kill. You can't believe God wants that. Such lust is a mental illness. Modern science—"

"Science?" Salvatore cried, cutting Balthasar to the quick. "What does 'science' know about the love of God or the joy of death? All that science tries to do is postpone Death. Cheat Death. Overcome Death. In the West, all of modern life so celebrates Science and Life, that it has tried not only to imagine a life without death but tries to create such a life here on earth. To me, it all has the stench of blasphemy. I tell you, Father, Science is the enemy of Death and, because of that, is the enemy of God and His will."

Death Blow

F ather Balthasar could not move. The ashen look on his face seemed, for the moment, to soften something deep within Salvatore. The young man's tone and demeanor, when he resumed speaking, were milder. "Of course, I don't mean you, Balthasar, because I believe you do look forward to being with our true Father, and I love you for it. But almost all of your tribe—you scientists, you doctors—want to preserve life, extend life, postpone death and, ultimately, to destroy Death. The real meaning of your medicine and your science is to make God unnecessary— to make this life here on Earth comfortable and desirable, more desired than the next. In the end, they look forward to the day when they themselves can create life and then make it eternal.

"But God wisely gave us death not only to encourage us to be good, but also to experience eternal life with Him— in Heaven, not on Earth. It is only through God, not science, that we believers will cheat death. But in all you say, Father, you celebrate this present life, when instead you should have infinite respect for Death. I tell you, *you should love Death!*"

"This is absurd, Salvatore! God is the God of the living, not of the dead!" Balthasar cried. "God is life itself. And He gave us stewardship over Earth. As Paul says, 'God gave us all things richly.' So, it is through science that we come to understand and use these blessings as best—"

"But we are not to act as God," Salvatore shot back. "We are simply to obey. And because He gave us all things richly, there's no reason to try to 'improve' on His creation. God is the way, the truth, and the life. But to reach that life, Father, we all must die."

Salvatore paused to stare at Balthasar, stunned and silent, as if pummeled by these words. But there was more. "Do you not see how Death is God's greatest gift to us?" Salvatore's voice was now as cold as a steel blade. "'Life' is the beginning of our trial here on Earth. Life is important only in that it leads to Death. Death is our entry into judgment. Death is when we are weighed and found worthy, or wanting. Death is paramount, for it leads to life everlasting, either with God in Paradise—or without Him in perpetual and just agony." Salvatore's voice reached a crescendo. "Don't fear Death, Balthasar. Don't reject it. Don't even try to postpone it. Welcome Death with open arms!"

Covering his ears with the palms of his hands and without asking for Father's blessing, Salvatore turned sharply and strode out of the sacristy.

Learning from Death

L ong after Salvatore had left the sacristy Balthasar remained rooted in his chair. Salvatore's rage had jolted him to the core, and Balthasar struggled as both priest and doctor to make sense of what had come to pass, but his troubled heart kept getting in the way. Surely his beloved boy had spoken with all the zeal of a teenager, one who is brilliant but not yet in full, adult command of how to deliver his thoughts. Perhaps he and Salvatore were not that far apart: One could surely concede that death is the way to eternal life and still celebrate life on Earth.

True, it was an old story that scientists were driven by the desire not only to understand nature but also to control it, to use knowledge to better the human condition. How did the words go? "Better living through chemistry"— a phrase he heard when he was young. Of course, medicine and pharmacy and psychiatry each worked to bring relief to this vale of tears. But if one looked deep enough, this was true of chemistry, physics, and biology as well—there was no field of study so "pure" as not to harbor the secret hope that it would be *the science* that might, that could, permanently change human lives for the better.

Yes, "better living through chemistry," Balthasar murmured, but he could feel his mind reeling.

It wasn't even Salvatore's words that so disturbed Balthasar. It's that he himself had indicated that the fanatical ideas about martyrs and murder Salvatore seemed to embrace with such fervor were the reflection of mental illness. In the heat of the argument, he had called Salvatore "absurd." How could it be that our revivified Lord would say an absurdity? Not only absurd, but wicked and absurd. Impossible! *Maybe I am the one who is absurd*, Balthasar wondered. *I have said foolish things.*

"Perhaps I have sinned," Balthasar whispered. "Rather than contradict my Lord, perhaps I should have been silent and listened." He slumped in his seat. "Perhaps the time for teaching Salvatore has truly come to an end and it is time for me to step aside, observe, and learn from what I've done."

The Company He Keeps

I t didn't take long for the seemingly sudden drastic change in Salvatore to become obvious to everyone in the convent, although its residents continued to do their best to attribute it to the throes of adolescence.

Salvatore had taken to leaving the convent grounds, particularly in the evenings, without mention of where he was going or where he had been, for increasing amounts of time. Soon there were nights when Salvatore didn't return home until nearly 5:00 a.m. In one respect these incidents lacked the character of teenage escapades. He was never drunk or tired, but always strangely energized. He would let himself in the back way, through a rarely used gate to which he had a key, and tiptoe up to his room. Salvatore seemed to think that no one knew that he was gone all night, and he tried to act as ordinary as possible. But nothing escaped the nuns.

The sisters were reluctant to tell Father Balthasar, however, especially since Salvatore had always made it back by dawn and was alert and generally polite. Given the circumstances surrounding his origins and his scholarly nature, they agreed collectively to allow Salvatore this relatively standard expression of youthful willfulness. But they remained watchful, even as there were some, such as Sister Maria, who privately harbored darker misgivings.

Then, one dawn, Salvatore didn't return. Father Balthasar confronted Mother Superior when the boy did not show up for an early morning theology recitation. "Where is he?"

"I don't know, Father. He's always back before five."

"*What?* Where does he go? How long has this been going on?"

The nun just wrung her hands.

Fear gripped Balthasar. He tried to calm himself by arguing that perhaps Salvatore was just about his Heavenly Father's business. After all, even Mary and Joseph lost sight of Jesus when they left him in the Temple, only to discover Him doing the right thing apart from them. But after their last confrontation, Balthasar could no longer deny that such reasoning was a lie.

Sister Luisa hurried over to them. "Forgive me, Father, for interrupting. Mother, we've received a call." She glanced nervously at the priest, then at Mother Margaret. "May— may I speak to you?"

"Is it about Salvatore?" Balthasar demanded.

"Yes, Father."

"Speak freely, Sister!" Mother Superior commanded.

Sister Luisa's voice was breathless. "It was a policeman. He said someone should come to the station to collect Salvatore."

Balthasar was so shaken that Sister Luisa was sent to ask Father Adrian if he would drive.

At the station they found Salvatore, sitting on a bench,

sullen. Captain Antonio Esposito took the priests aside and explained that Salvatore had been picked up with a bunch of Muslim hoodlums the previous evening, after having broken windows in a local synagogue and taunting the rabbi and his son. The other youths were being held in jail until the police and the rabbi decided what to do, but because they knew that Salvatore was an orphan who lived at the Vatican under Balthasar's care, they wanted to handle his circumstances more "discreetly."

"He's smart, and angry," the captain observed. "I'm not sure how he got mixed up with that group of trouble-makers, Father, but this is serious stuff."

"We'll talk to him," Balthasar managed to choke out. "Thank you for your discretion."

Father Adrian was shocked to see Balthasar walk over, grab Salvatore by the ear, and lead him firmly out the station door.

He turned to shake Captain Esposito's hand, then follow them out, but the man held on. He pressed a slip of paper into Adrian's palm: "Call me as soon as possible."

The Captain Talks

drian called Captain Esposito that afternoon. At
the captain's request, they met a few blocks from
the station.

"I didn't want to say everything I know to the old priest,"
the captain began, "but you look like you can handle it.
Then you can decide how much to tell the padre." He
scratched his chin. "Look, this wasn't the first time we've
crossed paths with Salvatore, but we had to arrest him this
time. At first, it was little stuff, stuff you chalk up to restless
teenage energy. So, you overlook some things. We were all
kids once. You know what I mean."

"Yes, but how long has this been going on?" Father Adrian
asked.

"He's been on our radar for over a year now."

Adrian raised his eyebrows.

"Yeah, for pranks, mostly, some rather mean-spirited,
but recently I've had a few of my more trusted men keep
their eyes on Salvatore. Officers who work the night detail
are always on the lookout for possible terrorist activity."

"*What?* Are you saying—"

"Look Father, I'm not calling the boy a terrorist. But he's

been running with a pretty rough crowd, all Muslim kids, and lately he's been with them a few nights a week. He's the youngest of the bunch."

Adrian sighed.

"It's strange, though," Captain Esposito continued. "The group seems to respect Salvatore. They look to him much more than they do some of the older ones. I understand he's pretty smart."

"Not as smart as he thinks he is," Adrian growled.

"There's something else. We've learned that the group he's running with is Shiite, from a pretty serious sect. They call themselves 'Twelvers.'"

"Do you mean like the leaders of Iran?" Adrian asked, stunned. "Twelvers believe that someday a descendant of Muhammad will unify all of Islam under one caliphate. From what I know their aim is to push aside the Sunni Muslims, completely obliterate Israel and the Jews, and subjugate all of Christianity."

The captain's face was grim. "We don't know who their leader is, but they definitely act as a group, under orders. And Salvatore is in cozy with them. You need to know that some in the group work at the Vatican, by the convent, as gardeners."

Adrian started.

"Including one of the worst. His name's Ali. He's about five years older than Salvatore, but the two seem tight. And if Salvatore keeps going like he's going, he'll land in more trouble than any of us want to imagine."

The two men talked further, shook hands, and parted with a commitment to stay in touch.

∞∞∞

It was with a somber heart that Adrian decided to carry this information to Balthasar, whom he found in his apartment, staring at the ceiling, and shaking.

He must hear everything, thought Adrian, pouring them each a glass of port. *I hope he can bear it.*

"As an example of what this group is capable of, Captain Esposito told me that a number of them were caught running through the ruins of the Forum with sharpened sticks. Balthasar, they were threatening people. One of the boys killed a small dog, then lifted its body—speared straight through—for everyone to see, laughing all the time! And it gets worse. The police believe they were targeting Jewish park visitors."

"Lord help us," Balthasar murmured. "Was Salvatore involved with the dog that was killed?"

"No, it looks like he was here in his room at the time, but I'm going to find out right now exactly what he knows."

Adrian found the boy in his room, then led him to a spare windowless study.

"What are you going to do," Salvatore sneered, "keep me here forever?"

"Don't be so dramatic," Adrian replied, too angry and concerned to take the bait. "We'll set up a cot and bring you meals," he added, before summarily locking Salvatore inside.

Adrian returned later with a cot and a small bowl of spaghetti with oil and garlic. He didn't mince words. "Do you know anything about a woman whose dog was killed in the park by the Forum?"

"What? *No.* Why would I?" Salvatore's face wore a strange defiant serenity. "And why would I care? Why should *you* care? Why would *anyone* care what happens to some Jewess and her stupid dog?"

With that, each now knew that they both knew. Adrian walked out, locking the door behind him.

Omar and the Fanatics

As 2025 wore on, matters grew more worrisome between Imam Omar and the increasingly radical elements in Rome's Muslim community.

Omar wisely decided that it was best that his occasional discussions with Balthasar and Adrian take place away from the Vatican. Instead they sat and talked on a bench surrounded by tourists at the edge of the Piazza del Popolo or in the mirrored gallery by the stupendous Velasquez portrait of Innocent X at the Doria Pamphilj Gallery.

"This portrait," Omar once observed, "perfectly depicts what I imagine your Pope Innocent himself to have been: ambitious, strong-willed, ferociously cold, and exceedingly cunning. I am forever amazed at how great painters can capture the nature, the very soul, of their subjects."

"I hope your description isn't genetic," Father Balthasar had responded with a grin. "The Doria and Pamphilj families have provided the Church with many prelates and princes. There's one even now, a descendant nephew of Innocent, raised some time back to the scarlet here in Italy."

"Now, Father," Omar chided. "Do I have to remind you of what you once told me: that, in your professional opinion, *everything* stems from the genetic?"

Regardless of topic, in these discussions both Adrian and Balthasar remained fascinated with how Omar wasn't as hard on Muslims as on Islam itself. Despite his troubles, Omar held his co-religionists dear—"which is why I am so concerned about Islam and all the false directions it has been moving, especially now," he told Adrian during their latest talk.

Ever mindful of their struggles with Salvatore, Adrian decided to probe Omar's thoughts about fanaticism and Islam.

"I think everyone has the causes of our current problems with Muslims wrong," the imam began. "With its usual sanctimony, the Left tells us that the radicalization of young Muslims is because of poverty or Israel or pervasive hopelessness. But none of that strikes me as persuasive. People in poverty may lash out, they may steal, they may even kill the rich, but people don't kill themselves because they're poor.

"Meanwhile, the Right is always going on about how this group or that radical figure uses social media to poison the minds of the young. The general public leans toward this view, too. I guess it's always easiest to blame some shadowy, charismatic figure for 'capturing' the imagination of our youth. But this is balderdash."

"With all due respect," Adrian responded, "it strikes me that the problem isn't circumstances or susceptibility to demagogic persuasion. The closer some people get to one particular religion—Islam—the more they degrade and enslave women, or torture and behead those who think differently. It seems to be something intrinsic—"

"Of course you mean that the more *some* Muslims accept a *certain false version* of Islam," Balthasar interrupted.

Omar was a bit surprised at Balthasar's anxious, almost offended tone. "No, my dearest friend, let's not sugarcoat the matter. What Adrian says, I believe, touches on the truth. There is something in the history of Islam, something in the tales of the Prophet and in the words of the Koran itself that point toward the obvious: today, Islam is the only religion whose adherents become more violent the stronger they believe."

"Let's be honest," Adrian added. "Islam has always been a 'conquering' faith."

"True," Omar nodded. "We Muslims say that while Christianity prides itself on having been spread by preaching, glorious Islam was spread by the sword!

"This is only partly true, of course. Christianity as well as Judaism was also spread by the sword, its adherents slaughtering not only Muslims and Jews, but also fellow Christians. But then this practice stopped! And this is part of what I hope to learn from both of you, through perhaps from Adrian most of all.

"What changed? Your Bible isn't different. The narratives of the life of Christ, the history of your saints—none of this has changed. You have kept your beliefs and your rituals, but Christians and Jews have changed their *behavior*. How? What do you Christians know that we Muslims do not?"

Before the Fountain

A week later, Adrian received a troubling voice message from Omar: "My friend, I must speak with you. Meet me tomorrow at 2:00 by the fountain in front of the Pantheon. Just yourself. We can walk and talk." Omar's voice hesitated. "If you would, please leave your collar at the Vatican. Dress, perhaps, as a tourist. I shall do likewise." Then, a pause. "One last request. I would like to bring my older son along. I want him to hear what you have to say… and I think he has something you should hear rather than dear Father Balthasar."

The next day as planned Omar introduced Adrian to his son, Imad. As the two shook hands he couldn't help but notice how different Imad—tall, handsome, fair—looked from his father. Omar's wife, God rest her, must have been lovely.

After the usual pleasantries, Adrian began by saying that he heard about the problem Omar had at his mosque the previous Friday, right after their last meeting at the gallery. "I saw in the paper that you had a suspicious fire at your house."

"It wasn't suspicious at all, my friend. Some ruffians firebombed our house while I was leading Friday prayers."

Adrian looked shocked.

"Yes, there was some damage," Omar continued, "but at least no one was at home. And of course, it was a frightening thing to happen, but we are not so easily scared silent, are we son?" He patted Imad on the shoulder.

Adrian looked around the busy piazza, studying the fountain with its spray and the bustling crowds of people before speaking again. "Omar, I'm puzzled. You're obviously a man in some danger. You have enemies; people bomb your home—yet you wanted to meet here, where there are a hundred local workers and a thousand tourists, where the chance of our speaking privately is nil."

Omar laughed, and Adrian could not decide if he were fearless or foolhardy. "I learned years ago when I was in Lebanon, from my friends in the protective services, that when you want to talk privately, never ever go to a quiet place, where people can overhear even a whisper. In this bustling piazza, no one will hear a word we say. We're less noticeable in this crowd, Adrian. We blend in better and have more privacy than in our own bedrooms."

It's amazing, thought Adrian, *how the most counterintuitive things can sometimes be so obviously true.*

Omar took Imad's hand and held him close on his left, asking Adrian to walk on his right. They walked slowly, casually. "I remain confused, Adrian, about Christianity. I know that the teachings of Jesus as recorded in the New Testament are more peaceful, more benign than the words of the Koran. I know as well that Jesus, whom we Muslims respect as a great prophet, was 'meek and gentle of heart.'

Yet, did he not say that he came not to bring peace but the sword? Jesus whipped people trading in the temple. He also said that he came to cast fire on Earth and wished before he died that the blaze were already ignited.

"Judaism is even worse. Hebrew scripture is full of the slaughter of enemies, including women and children. Old Testament Jews revel in the death of the Egyptians, they celebrate the murder of the Canaanites, they sing psalms asking God to shatter the jaws of their foes and break the teeth of those who oppose them. You want to see terrorism in the raw? Just read the exploits of Moses and Joshua against those they hated and whose lands they took. Like terrorists today, they said that God was directing them.

"But this is what continues to puzzle me: No matter what some cynics might say, today no religion is more peaceful, more, shall we say, 'liberal,' than Christianity or Judaism. How exactly did this happen? All I know is something happened that made them change, both of them."

"Well, that gets to the heart of the matter in a hurry, doesn't it?" Adrian said, somewhat surprised. "Maybe we should begin with the obvious. There's nothing in the New Testament that matches the brutality of some of the Koran's suras and verses, and there's nothing anywhere near as fierce as the stories of Muhammad, in which he is openly praised for his murderous ferocity. Christ chasing the money-changers from the temple with a handful of cords hardly compares to Muhammad ordering beheadings in his presence—then kicking the decapitated heads around with his feet."

"Your comparison is perhaps true," Omar replied, "but it

still doesn't explain the change in approach. For centuries, you Christians were terrorists yourselves. And the Hebrew Scriptures are just as violent and brutal as ours, but the Jews no longer act as their scriptural heroes once did. So, what pacified the Jews?"

"Papa, look at history," Imad interjected. "The Jews didn't change on their own; they're a broken people. They had their old ways *beaten* out of them."

"Yes," Adrian agreed. "The Romans scattered them, the Christians killed and exiled them, the Germans burned them."

"Father Adrian, I don't like this answer," Omar said. "I don't want my people to have to be crushed in order to become more civilized. Perhaps it's presumptuous of me, but, without changing one word of the Koran itself, I want to help my fellow Muslims to change their minds and change their hearts. When their minds and hearts are changed, they will then change how they read the Koran and how they act. Besides, the fact is that they—*we*—cannot be crushed. We Muslims have been slaughtering one another for centuries, and now there are more of us than ever. I fear that the more the rest of the world tries to crush us, the more raging and unstoppable the fanatics in our midst will become. No, without abandoning their sacred texts, Christians and Jews have truly changed from what their ancestors once were. I want to have some hint how we might start to do the same."

"What you want—to change the trajectory of Islamic fundamentalism over more than a thousand years—is easy to say, but impossible to achieve," Adrian responded.

Omar shook his head. "But, to take my example, it's clear to me that the Jews *have* actually changed their minds. They don't read their Bible the way their ancestors did. Some passages they read literally, but many others they do not. What's the guiding principle that leads the Jews to avoid eating pork but not to stone adulterers? Both were forbidden by God. Yet this command they keep and that one they ignore? How does one justify obeying God here and not there? And I could ask the same about the biblical things you Christians have kept and what you've discarded."

"Why do you think I can even begin to offer you an answer?" Adrian asked.

"Because Balthasar's told me a hundred times that you're the smartest historian and theologian he's ever met. My friend, those of us who want to reform our faith have too little time. What we have to learn is how to accept those teachings in the Koran that counsel toleration and charity and how to set aside those passages that teach hate. I need to do this not because our fanatics are terrorizing Christians or the Jews, but because the zealots of Islam are torturing, burning, and slaughtering my fellow Muslims."

A Place to Stand Together

"Let's think this through then," said Adrian. "We hear all the time that 'Islam needs a reformation the way the Christian Church underwent a reformation' as if it were some pearl of wisdom. But this was not what made us more tolerant. The Reformation was followed by the most brutal wars Christendom has ever witnessed. And it wasn't until after those wars were fought that a 'truce,' however fragile and imperfect, was called, and seems to be lasting."

"Well, I'm not about to preach jihad in the hopes that, when it's over, my people will have learned a lesson and stop fighting over religious matters," Omar responded. "Let's beat some sense into one another doesn't strike me as a winning formula. Besides, what if the more civilized side actually loses?" He reflected a moment, then added, "It was partly because of what Europe learned about fighting and armaments and organization during the religious wars that led it—once the backwater of the civilized world—to become 'the West,' the preeminent and most powerful force in history. For all our sakes, I'm not sure Westerners want the Muslim world to go down that path."

"Yes," Imad added after a long and somewhat painful pause. "But my father still wants to help our fellow Muslims start to act differently. And we don't want to see anyone hurt or killed, especially not in the name of God."

Omar drew his son close and the three of them walked until they found themselves outside the Tazza d'Oro cafe on the east side of the piazza.

"Shall we stop?" asked Omar.

Adrian nodded. "You find a spot for us to stand together."

He waved away Omar's offer to pay, and returned with three steaming espressos. "Let's talk a bit more about what happened in Europe after our horrific religious wars. It was then that peoples' minds turned toward other things, and new avenues, new ways of life opened up. Scientific exploration grew exponentially. Commerce expanded the world. Industry and technology followed. It seems, historically and over time, that the more they came to see themselves as scientists or merchants or bankers, and then as members of fraternal organizations, and then as municipal citizens, and then as soccer fans cheering for this or that team, the more people's attachments and loyalties have become mixed, varied, richer. It seems to me that when we have other outlets to satisfy our desire for meaning, the more thoughts of zealotry and fanaticism wear away. It was the birth of freedom that allowed for this in the West."

"I've heard all this before, Adrian," Omar replied, "and I don't believe it—at least not completely. When the West turned men's minds from God, saying 'Be free—follow your interests, follow your desires, follow your passions,' it brought about far more than commerce and inventions and medicine. It generated all the *new* zealotries, all the horrible political fanaticism of the last two centuries: colonialism, nihilism, Fascism, Communism. Everyone needs something to believe in, something to give their lives meaning, something higher they can attach themselves to, if nothing more than to make themselves more important in their own eyes. If we stop seeking God we don't always turn to science or soccer or doing good. Sometimes we are drawn to devilish things. How I can preach liberty and toleration and at the same time safeguard our faith?"

"I think you're belittling my point, Omar," Father Adrian began to object.

"I don't mean to, Adrian. But even if I wanted to import into Islam a greater respect for freedom and more worldly pursuits, I'm sure you can understand how difficult it is for a servant of God, as both of us are, to tell his congregation to be *more* worldly, to care *more* about the good things of this life than about zeal for God's will? Your sainted Pope John took a great gamble in saying that from now on the Church would 'open its windows' to the world, that it would make peace with modernity. Yes, he was praised for saying so. If I said it, I would be stoned."

"There have to be ways, Omar, of doing it with subtlety."

"When you find the words, my friend, please whisper them to me."

Throwing Stones

The three sipped their espresso in silence.

Finally, Omar spoke again. "One can read the Hebrew Bible and the Christian New Testament and find literally hundreds of passages that are either not true as written or which seem to contradict other parts of the text. For example, we know that God did not make the sun stand still in the sky so that Joshua's army might destroy their enemies."

"If He did, everyone would have been thrown off Earth and sailed into space," Imad said with an impish smile, "since that would actually mean that Earth had stopped, not the sun."

Adrian grinned. "Ah, you have an astronomer in the family."

Once again, Omar shook his head and patted Imad's shoulder. "To think, Adrian, this is the young man I hope will lead our congregation when I'm gone! Perhaps his sermons will be lighthearted enough that people come back to our mosque. Still, I must repeat the question: How can I teach my people the fullness of the Koran while setting aside the clearly false portions and, even more important, downplay the passages that teach violence while raising up the parts that preach charity and respect?"

Adrian knew it was impossible to answer with any hope of persuasiveness. "I can only speak about my own faith, Omar. Yes, the Bible, even the Gospels, contain contradictions. Was Mary a perpetual virgin or did Jesus have siblings? Is divorce always forbidden or are there exceptions, as parts of the text seem to say? The answer the Church has always given is that, when interpretation is unclear, as it often is, the Church herself will offer clarity. Who else is there? There must be one authoritative teacher, one final authority. This is why the *sola scriptura* of the Protestants is such a dead end.

"On what basis does the Church do this? It depends. Usually unclear or difficult passages are interpreted in light of what *is* clear. This means that the obviously central command to love our neighbor takes precedence over passages that seem to imply the opposite. And when the scriptural text is unhelpful, the Church digs into another resource: tradition.

"I know this hardly helps. And it helps Islam less than any other religion because, when all else fails, Christians can always point to the person of Christ, the gentle son of a carpenter, the man you described earlier as meek and humble. But you have a bloody warlord as your founder."

Omar seemed lost in his thoughts before answering. "I think you understand how hard my journey is." He sighed. "In one way, in Shi'a Islam, the situation is not far different than what you say about having one central source of teaching. They have a clear hierarchy. The Ayatollah Khomeini was considered by most Shi'a to be—how did you phrase it?—'the one authoritative teacher.' Many Shi'a even believed that the Ayatollah was the Twelfth Imam, the so-called Hidden Imam, who was hidden seventeen hundred years ago by Allah and who will return to fulfill Allah's final will, unify all Islam, and begin the rule of Islam over the entire world.

"Trust the Ayatollah to be our 'one authoritative teacher'? That way lies madness, Adrian, not safety. Look around at the fanatics. These people are truly barbarians, barbarians in the sense that nothing you say, nothing, could ever begin to make a difference. These are the members of Islam whom it will be the hardest, if not impossible, to reach. Reasons, arguments are beyond them. The truth burns in their hearts, and their ears are stopped and their minds impenetrable. And there's a wild and growing mob of them in the slums of Rome."

"All they talk about is how the Twelfth Imam is here and will lead them to victory," Imad added.

Omar shook his head. "So you see, I cannot go down the path of hoping for 'one authoritative voice,' since the one they choose may well be the worst in the world." He turned to his son. "It's time to for us to head back home and see what your brother is doing. Forgive me, Adrian, but Imad also needs to tell you something, something distressing. Something too hurtful, I think, to say to our friend Balthasar."

"I have a few friends who know these Twelvers my father is talking about," said Imad. He hesitated before plunging ahead, "They say that Salvatore hangs out with them.

They're really bad people. I just thought you should know. Sorry."

First the police captain, now young Imad… It seems everyone has opinions about Salvatore, and none of them good, Adrian thought. He kept his expression neutral and his voice steady in parting as he thanked Imad, and his father, for telling him and not Balthasar.

∞∞∞

When Omar and Imad returned home, Ahmed, their son and brother, showed them the broken window and the rock he had discovered among the pieces of glass on the kitchen floor. There was a note tied around the rock:

We hope you enjoyed your walk and espresso today.

Love and Hate

B y the old calendar it was Quinquagesima Sunday, the last Sunday before Lent and fifty days before Easter. Balthasar loved this particular Mass because it allowed him to preach a homily on his favorite reading from St. Paul. The Epistle assigned for the day came from the section of First Corinthians where Paul talks about the power of love. How love is more valuable than knowledge or faith; how love is patient, kind, humble. Paul wasn't Balthasar's favorite apostle, but here, the old priest thought, Paul got it all exactly right.

After Mass, Balthasar entered the sacristy and nodded at Salvatore, who stood and waited for him to change from his vestments into his ordinary clothes. The relationship between the two had chilled since the morning in the police station, although by all accounts to reach Balthasar's ears and by what he himself observed, Salvatore appeared to have decided to walk the straight and narrow. The old priest remained doggedly optimistic. The silence between them, however, left the room crystalline cold.

Salvatore broke the silence. "I do not know that I can learn from you any longer."

"Ah," Balthasar said, hopefully, "Because you've learned all I have to give you."

"No. Because you have nothing true to offer."

Balthasar put his hands on the back of a chair, then slowly walked around and sat.

"Even today, you talked not about God's will but only about your own desires. You never mentioned justice or doing God's work. You spoke only of humility and slavishness and being 'kind'—as if God commands weakness. Don't you see that mercy and sentimental love come after justice and repentance?" Salvatore's words were darts. "God loves the sinner who repents. But we are not to love evil, but to hate and destroy it—including those who refuse to convert or turn from evil ways. 'Any tree failing to produce good fruit will be cut down and thrown on the fire,' God says. Destroy these pictures of Jesus with his long locks and soft, sad eyes you have on the walls, Balthasar. See him as he is— with fiery eyes that declare 'I have not come to bring peace but a sword!'"

"Why must you cling to the darkest parts of the Gospels?" Balthasar cried.

"Why do you not?" Salvatore replied. "Don't you see how you've taken the soft parts and prettified them to put them on a pedestal and worship them? How you've done this for your own reasons, not God's? How you raise up the parts agreeable to your softness, because you love softness more than you love God?

"You talk about Christ's 'love.' Do you not see how ferocious his love was? How he withered the tree that did not bear fruit? How he called the leaders of the Jews, his

159

countrymen, 'snakes' and 'vipers'? How he declared that all who are rejected by his father fall into the pit of everlasting torment? Even the god of the perfidious Jews, whom you Christians say worshipped a stern god, was mild compared to Christ!"

"Hate the sin, but love the sinner," Balthasar objected weakly.

"The nuns taught me that lie when I was an orphan! Why do you not preach the truth, that God hates the sinner as well as the sin? Why else would He condemn the wicked to suffer in agony for all eternity? God doesn't end the lives of the wicked—He makes them cry in pain forever. Anyone who teaches otherwise teaches falsely.

"Still, you fail to see that love and hate are joined, Balthasar. You speak of love as sweet, mild, comforting. It is nothing, *nothing* like that. Even you know this, though you fail to honor it. 'Love is blind,' you rightly say. 'Love is not subject to reason.' 'Love is a fire that burns in the heart.' Yes—yes, a thousand times over! Consider the image of the Holy Spirit on Pentecost."

"The Holy Spirit is the very Love that the Father has for the Son!" Balthasar interjected.

"Yes," Salvatore shot back. "Yes! He *is* love. But this love didn't come down on that day the way you want to think of it, as a white dove. The Holy Spirit came down as *fire*. The Word of God speaks truly—FIRE! The Spirit came down as the thing that burns. The thing that purifies. The thing that enflames! The thing that destroys!

"Do you know what it means to be *enflamed*, Balthasar? It doesn't mean to study or to analyze or to be reasonable.

It means to have the all-consuming passion of fire. Love is passion itself, with all its cleansing fury."

"God is Love," Balthasar broke in.

"Yes," agreed Salvatore. "God *is* Love—and Love is Fire. God is also reason, for everything He says is His, and is therefore right and true. But it is a reason enflamed, a reason that doesn't ask for agreement but demands obedience!

"And so, all the vain talk of your philosophers who taught that reason should rule our passions was exactly that: vanity. They were just trying to tame the love of Christ. But love is not reason, and the love of God is fierce beyond our understanding! Love distains all the comfort and softness you falsely claim the Prophet Christ taught. Love builds up, love possesses, love destroys, and love kills!" Salvatore's voice reached a fever pitch. "The love of God is hatred of everything else! Not to hate wickedness, not to hate the wicked, is not to love God.

"Your nuns, your philosophers, your pacifists, your saints with birds on their arms—you have all lost sight of what you should love and what you should hate, *what you should hate with all your heart*. You have made your Christianity soft and meek. You have made your Christ into a faggot!"

Leaving Balthasar stricken and speechless, Salvatore strode out of the sacristy and toward the courtyard, which was flooded with the new day's light.

Omnia Vincit Amor

Father Adrian was walking from the refectory toward the chapel, where he always stopped to pray before embarking on the day's work in earnest. Suddenly Salvatore was there before him, standing in the shadow between two brightly lit arches.

"What do you think Virgil meant when he said *Omnia vincit amor*—Love will conquer everything? What do you think Augustine meant when he said there was only one brief law: Love, then do what you will?" Salvatore demanded, without salutation.

"I'm not sure," Adrian replied, surprised but not shaken by Salvatore's abrupt questioning. "What do you think they meant?"

"You're not sure?" Salvatore shot back with a sneer. "*Not sure!* Well, of this I am sure: Virgil didn't mean that softness and sentimentality will beat back darkness and evil. Neither rationality nor sentimentality has all that much power. They certainly don't have the power to conquer."

"Is that what you think, Salvatore?"

"Yes. True love is fierce, single-minded, passionate devotion. A devotion so intense that it mows down everything in its path. Love conquers all only if we mean the unquenchable, unstoppable love of God, a love that heeds no other voice but His."

"So, you've been reading and reflecting on love these days?" Adrian said.

"Yes, and I think Augustine didn't mean that all we need to do is be nice and kind, as if that makes everything right in God's eyes. He meant that true Love—the ferocious, unquenchable desire for God and devotion to His word and His kingdom—to act from this Love is all we need to do to gain eternal life. This Love makes all we do beautiful before God, even if the world condemns us or calls us mad."

"And what exactly is the purpose of this study, Salvatore?"

"Do you not see how the Muslim world grows and grows? Does it grow because Muslims preach softly and speak sweetly to every living thing? No, it grows because their martyrs have love sufficient to renounce everything but God and His will. And it grows because they love enough to die for God and God's ways."

"They also seem to love murder, too," Adrian said, uncowed by Salvatore's ferocity.

"No, it's not 'murder,' although it *is* killing," Salvatore acknowledged. "Your Pope Benedict was correct to say that the Muslims want to spread their faith by the sword. And why not? Our God ordered all nations everywhere to come to Him. If it is necessary to kill and be killed to spread the word, then the love of God says *so be it.*"

Salvatore started to walk away.

"Are you trying to convince me that the ends justify the

means, Salvatore," Adrian called after him, "or are you trying to convince yourself?"

Salvatore paused and turned. "In doing God's will, *all* means are just," he said, his lips smiling, his eyes both ice and fire. "Love demands that we do whatever Love demands. Besides, if the ends don't justify the means, Adrian, then tell me what does?"

The Reckoning

Father Adrian raced to the sacristy, where he found the old priest slumped in a chair. "He's a monster, Balthasar—a damned evil animal!"

Balthasar raised his head. "Don't say that, Adrian. I've been over it and over it in my mind. Maybe Salvatore is right and we are wrong. Maybe he's come to tell us that we have been too soft. That we've made life and comfort and science our gods."

"Goddamn it, Balthasar, Salvatore is no more the reincarnation of Christ than I am!"

"All I know is that I helped bring into this life the person whose blood was on the Shroud," Balthasar replied wearily, as if he'd been repeating this to himself. "And we all know that that person was the Christ. We know it as firmly as—"

"You're being completely irrational," Adrian snapped. "We do *not* know that it's Christ's image on the Shroud. At least *I* don't."

Balthasar's eyes flashed, but he didn't argue.

"For the safety of the nuns we serve, for your own protection, Balthasar, we have to send Salvatore away. Let him live among his hoodlum friends, where he wants to be—and belongs."

"No!" Balthasar cried. "It would destroy his mother—and I couldn't bear it. I beg you, let's talk to him first. We must tell Salvatore the truth about his origins—that he may reflect upon it and be changed!"

Balthasar became so distraught that Adrian finally relented. *But no matter what Balthasar says*, Adrian told himself, *I'm afraid that all of this will end the same way.*

Confrontation

After the old priest finally calmed down, Adrian walked him to his apartment and went to find Salvatore, who was pacing the courtyard, seemingly deep in thought. Adrian expected another confrontation, but the young man followed him without question or objection. He wasn't wearing the now familiar surly look on his face. Nor did he appear smug or tense or ready to argue. In fact, Salvatore's body was relaxed and his face blank as he sat down across from the priests.

"Salvatore," Balthasar began somewhat shakily, "the time has arrived for us to speak with you about yourself. I want to share something with you about your background, how you came to us: Sister Maria is your mother."

Salvatore stared directly at Balthasar. "I know."

Balthasar trembled. He and Adrian exchanged looks. "There is more you need to know. After you were conceived but before you were born, I took DNA off the Shroud of Our Lord in Turin, and imbedded it in your growing embryo."

Salvatore did not react, and Balthasar pressed on. "Sister Maria, your mother, does not know this. Only the three of us in this room know. And I am certain that you are the rebirth of Our Lord, Jesus Christ."

Adrian moved to interrupt and Balthasar paused, but when Salvatore still showed no reaction he continued. "I know that when Christ—you—first came that he came unto his own, as it's written, 'His own received him not.' I have tried to receive you openly, to the best of my ability, but I don't know where I've gone wrong. I don't understand you or what you are asking me to do. Help me understand."

Without responding to Balthasar, Salvatore turned to Adrian. "And who do you say I am?"

"I say that there's no way in hell you're Christ returned. If by any chance you're the spawn of what's on the Shroud, then what's on that cloth is the very opposite of Our Lord. But what I really think is that Father Balthasar is deluding himself. You, Salvatore, are the product of a saintly woman raped by some filthy low-life scum."

There was a tense pause, but Salvatore only turned back to Balthasar, his gaze sly yet placid. "Once again, Adrian is half-wrong, but still more correct than you, Balthasar. I know that Sister Maria is my mother because my father told me. He was, as Adrian said, filthy scum."

"No!" cried Balthasar, "I know what I did and—" but Salvatore silenced him with a gesture of his hand.

"Ali, my comrade, brought him here, to the gardens, to meet me. His name was Rahman. Rahman lived by stealing and found his pleasure not in prayer or study but in drunkenness and rape. Italian women, tourists, school girls."

"A disgusting man," Adrian said, repulsed, "but how do you know this Rahman is your father?"

"Rahman said that he liked virgins best. He even bragged

about raping a nun while his friends watched. It happened a long time ago, near the place where the migrants gather during the day. As I watched Rahman boast about what he'd done, I saw my own face."

Balthasar, horrified, sickened at Salvatore's words.

"Yes, I saw myself—but I could not see my father. I could only see the man who defiled my mother. To her great shame she is still defiled, but he is the worse one. He bragged that he was a great Muslim, the maker of Muslim babies, but I saw only refuse, just as Adrian said. So, I told Ali that just like garbage, Rahman should be disposed of."

"What do you mean by that?" Adrian asked.

"Ali took Rahman back to his apartment, where, of course, he became drunk. Then Ali administered the Holy Sacrament of Death, at my request." Salvatore's voice remained steady. "A sharpened shiv to the neck, just as one might bleed a pig. Rahman had his pleasures in this world; now for all his sins, he is in agony forever, in Hell."

There was a terrible pause before Salvatore focused his steel gaze on Balthasar. "Unlike Adrian, you are mistaken in many ways. You claim that you don't understand me, that you have tried to receive me but that I have rejected you. What you cannot see is that I have come unto my own, and my own *have* received me. You are confused, but I know who I am, why I came into the world, and what is my mission."

The room fell silent. Salvatore stood still, as if transfixed. Then his mouth began to move and words poured out—passionate, terrible words, though uttered in a monotone, as one under hypnosis, or in a trance, might speak.

Revelation

"I am the one the servants of Allah call the Twelfth Imam. I was first born in your year 868. Two hundred and thirty-six years had passed since the death of the Prophet, peace be upon him, and over two hundred years since the city of Jerusalem was given to the slaves of Allah for the eternal glory of His name.

"In the spring of my seventh year I was hidden by Allah, not in death, but hidden, even from my relatives. Then, for 220 years I was hidden by Allah; I was with Him and I did not age. I was sent back to this life in your year 1070, when later I made my way to Jerusalem, where I was told I would begin my work and then be tested.

"This first return was necessary for the strengthening of the children of Allah and ordained by Allah as the first step that would lead to the end of days.

"Jerusalem was then the pearl of Allah, radiant and serene. All followers of the Book lived there—slaves of Allah, children of Abraham and Moise, followers of Issa—the son of Miriam, the prophet whom you call Jesus the Christ. I was sent to strengthen the slaves of Allah in purity and to prepare them for what was to come.

"In 1099 of your calendar I was living in Jerusalem, teaching openly, when those who bore the cross of infamy on their chests, took the holy city. Even though I was not yet thirty, I had been accepted in Jerusalem and beyond as *imam*—teacher, leader, servant, guide—as the blood of Muhammad, as the remnant of Allah, as the one who would rise, as the Hidden One who had come.

"Enflamed by their Christian pope and their ravenous kings bent on conquest, the animal hordes of Europe had been sent to Jerusalem to steal the pearl from the treasury of Allah and from the hands of His servants. These 'crusaders' sought me out especially, as the most spirited and steadfast of all the slaves of Allah. In the summer of 1099 I was taken, beaten, tortured, and killed.

"Everyone was killed. Jews who had lived among us were killed without mercy—their men hacked to pieces, their women cut open, their smallest children lifted on swords or thrown in the air for sport and caught on the ends of pikes. The 'crusaders' claimed they did this to avenge the slaughter of the innocents.

"Even Christians descendant from the disciples of Issa, who had lived peaceably in Jerusalem for a thousand years, who ran to greet the animal hoard, throwing themselves happily at the feet of the cross-bearers—even they were slaughtered amid cries of 'Jewess lover!' and 'Friends of the infidel Saracen!' Asked if they knew of Alexius, if they said yes, they were killed; if they said no, they were called liars and beaten until they said yes. Then they were killed.

"From among so many thousand slaughtered two were tortured and crucified: the high priest of the Jews and me.

"The head rabbi and I were captured and, before the Dome of the Rock, before the swinish crowds of cross-bearers, we became actors in a play.

"We were brought outside the wall of the great mosque tied together, standing in a mule cart covered in palm fronds. We were pushed out of the cart and brought before a Jew-child dressed as a great ruler.

"The cross-bearers made him stand on a high platform and say, 'Shall I free these two who deny your Christ, or shall I crucify them to pay for the sins of their people?'

"'Crucify them! Crucify them!' the cross-bearers shouted, snorting and prodding like beasts about to stampede. They spit on us and beat us with sticks, and then, before the filthy crowd, their ringleaders tied us to poles and took turns whipping us with leather straps and cords studded with nails. A crown made of thorns was pushed into my head, but they would not crown the other because he was a Jew.

"In playing out this mockery, they said they were avenging the death of Christ and gaining God's favor.

"And then the Jew and I were crucified. They hammered nails into my wrists—as they had learned from the Syrians, who learned how crucify criminals from the Romans centuries before—and one nail into both my feet. They stripped me naked, hung me on the cross, and cursed me.

"As I neared death, they cut my side open with a pike, so I would bleed like an animal after the hunt. They broke the Jew's legs with a hammer, and when he was dead, cut out his eyes, as they said was done to the thief they mistakenly say was hanged on the tree next to the Prophet Issa, a prophet they stupidly think Allah allowed to be killed.

"The rabbi's corpse they fed to dogs and birds. *No burial for the Jew-killer of Issa!* Me, they said they would bury. My people and I were not Christ-killers, but thieves and ravagers of Christ's holy property, sacred land. 'It is up to our God, in His mighty judgment, to raise you up, you and your kind, either to forgive you or punish you forever.'

"So they took my body and allowed three pious servants of Allah they kept alive as slaves to anoint me with spices and wrap me in linens, again in mockery of what was done in legend to Issa. And the brutish hoards stood as witness as I watched from above, secure under Allah's protection.

"They put my shrouded corpse in a cave, as they said was done with Issa. On the third day, the chief of the 'crusaders,' Baldwin, brother of Godfrey of Bouillon—Baldwin, who soon would take the title of King—came with some followers and unshrouded my nakedness, crying 'God is appeased!' Baldwin mocked me, spitting and saying, 'Our Lord Jesus Christ rose after three days, but Allah has left his servant to stink in a cave.'

"Later, Baldwin would sell the cloth that swathed my murdered body to the high priests of the Church in Constantinople, proclaiming it the bloodstained Shroud of Issa, which he had discovered in a hidden place in the Church of the Sepulcher. It fetched a king's ransom. My body itself was tossed atop a pile of corpses in a ravine.

"From that day till now I have lived in the peace of Allah, until restored to life by you, Balthasar, magician and unwitting servant of Allah, Allah the Merciful, Allah the Compassionate."

DEVASTATION

Slaughter

The two priests sat frozen, Adrian horrorstruck, Balthasar weeping, as the person they had known as Salvatore rose and left the apartment. Neither moved from the spot until they heard wild shouting in the hallway outside. Adrian was rushing for the door when four ragged young men burst into the apartment. They grabbed the priests and dragged them to the Vatican gardens overlooking the campo that adjoins the art galleries.

Adrian reached out to steady Balthasar, who was about to collapse. The sudden horror of the scene was too much to bear as he pointed speechlessly to the sisters of the Convent of St. Paul. The nuns were guarded at knifepoint as they huddled, weeping and terrified, near to where Salvatore stood, calmly waiting for the priests to arrive.

Salvatore gestured for them to consider the campo below, where hundreds of young Muslim men swarmed, swaggering and shouting crazily.

They looked, and learned what was inciting the mob. Three youths stood before the frenzied crowd carrying the severed heads of Omar, Imad, and young Ahmed held high on pointed sticks.

Adrian was ashen, but stood ramrod straight. Balthasar retched.

The mob began cheering as the nuns of the orphanage, wailing pitifully, were forcibly processed before them, followed by a line of small orphans, tied with ropes and pushed and kicked along by their captors. From down on the campo, the nuns were led up to the top of the ridge and made to stand with Sister Maria and the other nuns from her convent, so that all could be forced to watch the morbid spectacle as it slowly played out.

The gates the mob had entered were being guarded by boys with AK-47s ready to shoot the police now arriving with shields and armored cars. As the police frantically attempted to assess the situation, Ali—the young man Salvatore had subdued and had chosen to murder his father Rahman—sprinted to the top of the ridge to stand beside Salvatore.

He raised his arms and the mob fell silent. "In the name of Allah, most compassionate, most merciful," Ali called out, "today, to you, the Mahdi, the One who was Hidden, is now revealed!"

At these words, the mob let loose a cry that echoed throughout Rome.

"Today, the one chosen by Allah, the descendant of Ali, of Hussein, and of Muhammad—may peace be forever upon him—has come to begin Allah's reign and restore His rule over all the lands which are rightfully His. Today, the infidels who defame the name of Issa will be destroyed. Today, the blasphemers and apostates who spit when they repeat the words of the Holy Koran will know their fate."

With that, Omar's head was pulled from its pike and tossed and kicked about amid triumphant jeers, until abandoned in a ditch as Salvatore, the so-called Mahdi, descendant of Hassan, of the lineage of the family of Muhammad, stepped forward to speak.

"In the name of God, the merciful, the compassionate. There is no God but Allah and Muhammad is His Messenger.

"I have been sent to you by Allah. I am the true Mahdi, the Twelfth Imam, the Hidden One, the Long-Awaited." The voice of the mob rose up at these words and became so deafening that nothing more could be heard for what felt like hours.

The Mahdi raised his arms and waited for the roar to fade. From where he and Balthasar were being held nearby, Adrian noticed a long blade glint at his waist. Finally, the Mahdi spoke again.

"I have been sent to destroy those who say 'God is Three.' I have come to put an end to the corruptors of the words of the Holy Prophet Issa, also called the Christ. Issa stands over me, urging me to cut the tongues from all who have profaned his teachings and his holy words.

"I have come to claim for Allah this holy city. Today, we will take this great church as once we took over the greatest of all churches and made it into Allah's mosque in Istanbul. Today, we will cleanse this church, and from it send you out with knives and swords to cleanse the world of the mother of Crusaders, of the filth called Christianity.

"We will destroy the dogs who have made that religion a religion of sin. We will bring justice to those who tried to steal the land won by Allah for His servants. We will bring justice to the worshippers of Allah driven from their homes in Spain and Italy and all Europe. We will kill the Jewish pigs who have desecrated Jerusalem, the holy land of Allah."

At these words, Sister Maria broke from her cheering captors, rushed past Adrian and Balthasar, and threw herself at her son's feet, frantically begging him to stop.

Unmoved, the Mahdi nodded at one of his thugs, who approached, yanked Maria from her son, and threw her over the ledge. She landed twenty feet below to shrieks and cheers, her body broken and crumpled.

"God in Heaven, save us!" Balthasar cried out—and one of the young guards holding him turned to the old priest, who always said he would never ask God to bend to his will, and struck him so fiercely in the mouth that he reeled backward, choking on blood and teeth.

Only Adrian stood silent and rigid, held fast by two of the Mahdi's followers. As his captors watched the melee below, Adrian broke loose and lunged at Salvatore. Grabbing the knife at the boy's waist, Adrian held the point below his ear. He pushed the point in just enough to begin to draw blood. Ali and the bodyguards froze and the crowd screamed louder than ever.

Knowing he had seconds to act, Adrian spoke quickly: "Balthasar believed you to be Christ returned. You think you're the 'Hidden Mahdi' sent by Allah to usher in the reign of Islam. But I know exactly what you are: the bastard son of a street criminal, conceived in rape. In no religion are you holy. *In every religion you are nothing but a pig.*" Eyes flashing with fearless defiance as the guards jumped him,

Adrian drove the knife up through the soft part of Salvatore's neck into his brain.

The guards stabbed Adrian again and again until his body was as lifeless as their leader's. Ali leapt at Balthasar, grabbed him by the hair, and sliced his neck above the Adam's apple with his blade, sawing through the old priest's spine until his head was severed from his body.

Ali turned to the stunned crowd and shouted triumphantly, "The Mahdi did what he was assigned—he brought the reign of Allah back to the world." He raised his bloody arms. "We now conquer that world in his name! Do as you have been instructed!"

The bloodthirsty mob moved from the grassy area where it had gathered and swarmed the front of St. Peter's, confronting and disarming the Roman police in the piazza with the sight of the terrified orphans and nuns who'd been dragged along at knifepoint. The mob then thundered into St. Peter's, where every soul they encountered was slaughtered.

When all were dead, the murderers turned their rage on the church itself, toppling statues, slashing paintings, overturning tabernacles, and smashing pews. Tripping over the bodies of the dead, they took their knives to the frescos and mosaics and where they encountered images of saints or prophets gouged out the eyes. Stabbing and hacking, they raged joyously until the great monument to evil was destroyed and their own bodies were drenched in the blood of the wicked.

As the sun rose higher, the great Basilica of St. Peter was taken.

The Occupation

Pope Clement, pale and shaking, stood rooted at his window staring at the aftermath of the massacre in the campo and the gardens. No matter that his quarters were protected by a dozen Swiss Guards and three carabinieri on detail to the Vatican from Rome. The Holy Father was terrified.

The uprising and destruction had seemed to play out in slow motion, yet unstoppably fast and in all directions. Even as the "cleansing" of the great basilica was raging a contingent of Muslims armed with AK-47s was invading the papal quarters. Neither the tall, beautiful Swiss in their extravagant uniforms nor the Roman police armed with uzis were any match for this Kalashnikov-bearing army. Led by Muslim gardeners and cooks employed at the Vatican, the invaders knew exactly where to go.

Within seconds, those guarding the pope's quarters were mowed down.

Ali had sent his first lieutenant, Hassan, not to kill Clement but to demand his surrender. There was nothing—not nuns, not even children—that could compare to holding the pope hostage.

After killing the guards, Hassan's men kicked in the door, and Hassan entered the pope's quarters alone. Kneeling in a corner, trembling and praying, was the Holy Father, still in his bedclothes. Hassan walked over to him, lifted him by his hair, and stared into his face.

The hostage appeared to be neither brave nor formidable. He was elderly, smaller than his captor by half a foot, and Hassan was disgusted to see the old man's face wet with a coward's tears. This was the leader of billions of infidel Christians? Still, he would be useful.

Hassan pushed the old man into a chair and looming over him, spoke. "You are a prisoner, a hostage, of the Army of Liberation of the Twelfth Imam. I am Hassan, second to Ali, our leader, who—the Mahdi, the Twelfth Imam, the Hidden One, the Long-Awaited, having been murdered by one of your own—is now ruler of all the dominions that once belonged to you, the fallen leader of the infidel Christians."

Clement gaped.

Hassan grabbed and shook Clement. "Do you hear and understand?"

Reeling, Clement nodded.

Hassan shoved a paper into the pope's hands. "You will read this statement within the hour from the balcony of these quarters that acknowledges that Ali now commands the Vatican state and all connected to it. You will announce that you are safe and unharmed in the custody of Allah's servants, who deign to let you live—as long as you cooperate with us completely." Hassan ignored Clement's gasp and continued. "You will also state that any attempt to take this city from our hands will be met with immovable resistance—and that you as well as all women and children we hold captive will be beheaded. Do you understand?"

Weeping, Clement nodded.

Hassan then ordered Clement to strip and put on simple papal garb, but without miter or crown or skullcap. "Bareheaded, infidel!"

When the pope had dressed, Hassan ordered him to stand and read the statement.

Clement began to read, his hands trembling. Then he looked at Hassan. "I cannot read this to my people as written."

Hassan turned scarlet. "*No?*" He slapped Clement with the back of his hand.

The Holy Father staggered. Then he slowly, visibly gathered himself and, in a voice containing neither fear nor rancor, said that he needed to instruct and calm his flock, not threaten them. "I will not contradict what is written, but I need to say more. I must also say that God demands of us peace, not retaliation and not conflict, and that this is the only path to resolution."

Hassan was stunned. Who would expect this sudden fortitude from such a frail and brittle old man? As he scrambled for a response to regain charge of the situation Hassan remembered, in studying the enemy to prepare for this day, certain things he had learned about the person who called himself Clement XV.

Clement had been pope for just over a year and no one seemed to know quite what to make of him. He had been serving in the Vatican's administrative leadership when he was elected by a college of cardinals that Francis, over time, had packed with his allies. Still, the scandals of sex and abuse had so clouded the final years of Francis's papacy that the College of Cardinals took weeks before they could reach even a bare consensus. While Clement's stand on doctrine was believed to be fully in line with Francis's, the softness of his manners, his willingness to listen to all sides, and his non-confrontational demeanor set the two apart.

Still, what did Clement mean when he said that God demands all Christians to put aside conflict? *Is this an act of surrender—or a trick?* Hassan wondered. *Impossible! He is my hostage. He has no power.*

The old man sitting before him seemed simple, without guile. Hassan decided that Clement was not trying to bargain for his own freedom. There was a quiet peace about the man that was unsettling, as if he knew that his attempt to call for calm and avert further bloodshed might well be his last, but greatest, act.

Hassan surprised himself. He decided to let events play out as Clement suggested.

"Do not cross me, old man, or I will kill you as you speak!" Hassan whispered, for in his heart he also knew, *Ali will kill us both if I fail him.*

Conversion

Even before Pope Clement was led onto the balcony to address the world, the bodies of the many murdered were already being thrown out beyond the walls of the Vatican as the Mahdi's—now Ali's—followers were systematically killing every man and boy discovered within Vatican City, already "re-christened" the Capital of the Muslim Ummah in the West.

Any old woman taken hostage in the first frenzy was kept alive, but to what purpose and fate was not revealed. Not so for the younger women who had been captured.

Some of these were women who lived with their families in Vatican City or came in from Rome to hear Mass before going to work within the Vatican as secretaries or bookkeepers. But for the women now huddled with the nuns of the Convent of St. Paul and the orphanage—all trying together to soothe the terrified children and infants in their midst—the lives they once lived were gone.

They were herded at gunpoint into one of the galleries in the museum area, where Ali and six of his armed men stood waiting. "It is not your goodness, but through the beneficence of Allah that your lives have been spared," Ali told them. "In this small city, all who live within its walls must serve Allah. You must choose. Convert, or there will be death."

Amid the frightened weeping, several of the nuns cried out: "Convert? Kill me then!" "I will never abandon my faith!" "Dear Lord Jesus, I offer my soul to you."

Ali smiled coldly. "You mistake my meaning. It is not *you* who will die. Each woman will come before me in turn. If you refuse to convert, we will kill one of these children before your eyes."

Weeping became wailing as Sister Margaret, the Mother Superior, spoke out in a firm, clear voice. "It is not allowed for us to commit even a venial sin willingly. To deny our Lord and betray our faith is the very worst of sins. We cannot commit it."

But even as these words were uttered, some of the nuns from the orphanage cried out in dissent. "We are willing to die, but we cannot cause another's death! For the sake of the children, please Reverend Mother, do as he says!"

"I will not," Mother Superior repeated. "I cannot!"

Ali stepped forward and grabbed a small boy no more than two years old from the arms of the woman who clung to him. He held the sobbing child by one ankle and slit his throat.

The Reverend Mother slumped to her knees.

Ali put a bloody hand upon her bowed head. "I ask again. Who among you will not convert?"

Cowering and tears were the only answer.

Addressing the Faithful

Bareheaded and barefoot, a cord tied at the waist of his simple robe, the Holy Father stood on his balcony, Hassan and his henchmen, fully armed, to his left and his right.

Unlike all other days, today Pope Clement did not address an adoring crowd of pilgrims, but the Muslim rabble screaming and waving and cursing him from below. Every cell phone, every transmitting device, every video camera the mob held high carried his words worldwide.

"In the name of God and with all my heart I repeat the words of Christ to his disciples and to each and all of us: 'Peace be with you.'

"The entire world has by now seen today's events: terror and death beyond description. Every Christian and all people of good will—myself as pope above all—must do all we can to end this massacre."

Hassan lifted his rifle at these words, but Clement pressed forward. "I beg any Vatican guards still alive and all the police of Rome, please do nothing that will lead to greater bloodshed. If we wish to end conflict, we must not be the makers of it. Peace is what is demanded of us. Peace is our Lord's wish and command to us. For only as peace-makers we will be called Children of God."

Weak fool, Hassan thought, lowering his rifle.

"The witness we are called to bear is the witness of peace," the pope continued calmly. "In the midst of conflict, we will find neither understanding nor justice. We say, so easily, that without justice there can be no peace. But the reverse is also true, perhaps more true: Without peace there can never be lasting justice.

"Brothers and sisters in Christ, death is not to be countered with more death, injustice is not stopped by vengeance, and conflict is not abated through more conflict.

"Are we not instructed to put aside the sword? In the name of Christ, cease all fighting. With prayer, with calm, and with understanding, let us have faith that all can and will be resolved.

"I am old, and my own life is as nothing. I have no fear of death. But what is there in this world that is worth this continued killing? Is it property? Is it buildings? Is it art? What can be balanced against the death of innocents? I beg everyone who hears my voice, please, draw back.

"As you put down your weapons, please know that I refuse to see myself as a hostage, but rather as a ransom. A ransom given as the assurance of peace. Peace among men; peace between faiths. Our Lord Jesus Christ did not come to bring condemnation but to bring peace. I give myself voluntarily not as the hostage, but as the guarantor of peace.

"I urge all people of all faiths to pray for peace among all parties in this conflict. Let us remember, above all, that as we ask for forgiveness so we forgive those who trespass against us. Brothers and sisters, pray for me, pray for my captors, and pray for all of God's Holy Church."

A small smile flashed across Hassan's face as he watched Clement drop the paper containing the statement he was supposed to have read and skulk back to his quarters. The old man's feeble words about peace and the timid call for Christian surrender were infinitely better than what he and the other liberators had prepared—or expected.

Expansion

By the next day, every person left living in what had been Vatican City had sworn an outward oath that there existed no God but Allah and that Muhammad was his Prophet.

With that, as had been planned, all the younger women were distributed among Ali's holy soldiers to become their wives or concubines and most of the older women were kept as servants, with a few assigned to watch over the hostage children, held for some future use.

Ali knew what every Islamist had known and been acting on for years: that the conquest of the West would only be achieved through indirect threat. Brave men and women could always be found who would face their own death, often no matter how gruesome, to defend and uphold their beliefs. But threaten them with harm inflicted on others—make their steadfastness the cause of suffering or death, especially of the youngest—and watch such fearless individuals surrender everything. This was the meaning of terror in the West, and the Achilles heel of Christianity.

"The slaughter of innocents is a surer road to victory than the killing of our enemies," Ali reminded his followers as they carried the bloody, manipulative scenario begun with the hostage nuns and orphans.

Beyond the walls of the Vatican young Christian women were captured off the streets of Rome or taken by force from their houses. They were carried back to the occupiers and declared their "wives." Each Muslim who had taken part in the capture of the Vatican was then given his choice of a slave-bride. This soon became a most attractive tool to recruit new jihadists.

And so, in the tumultuous days following the capture of the Vatican, a number of Muslim neighborhoods in and around Rome declared themselves to be under the rule of Ali. No police officer who was not a faithful Muslim himself was permitted to enter these enclaves, or guard the perimeters of what was becoming an expansive Muslim state within greater metropolitan Rome.

As terrorists had discovered when they began taking over vast areas of the Middle East, what is captured can often be sold. As ISIS had survived in part by selling for large sums the oil they had stolen, so the terrorists who captured the Vatican quickly discovered the untold profits to be had not in destruction but in selling off the Holy See's Raphaels, Caravaggios, Titians, and other treasures. The Sistine Chapel was systematically picked apart and sold. The forearm and hand of Christ broken off the Pieta, salvaged from the remains of St. Peter's Basilica, was reputedly purchased for fifty million Euros by a private Asian "collector." The money available for fighting this new jihad made the past support of the Saudis or the Iranians seem, by comparison, insignificant.

Complicity

To the Catholic world at large—a world that expected braver words, words of reassurance, words, above all, of strength and defiance even in the face of sure death— Clement's address was seen as the most cowardly and incomprehensible speech in human memory. Among the hierarchy of cardinals and bishops worldwide, what the pope said not only turned their world upside down, it elicited dismay and even scandal. One African cardinal, no friend of either the previous or current pope, stepped forward to announce that if Pope Clement lacked the courage to defend the Church from her enemies, or offer himself for the good of the Church, he no longer deserved his title. He and his fellow African cardinals, he said, were preparing a call for a new conclave to consider declaring the Chair of St. Peter to be empty.

Joining with the entire hierarchy of Poland and Hungary, the Cardinal Archbishop of Milan followed suit. Just as Benedict had resigned his office when incapacitated, the Milanese cardinal wondered before all the world if Clement had effectively "resigned," since he seemed incapable of carrying out even the most basic functions of his office:

As a captive, Clement was unable to convene his bishops, minister to his diocese, administer the sacraments, or even celebrate Mass. Speaking for many within the European hierarchy and beyond, the cardinal archbishop offered the buildings and capacious possessions of his archdiocese to house the remnant of the Vatican curia and become, with his help and under his guidance, the new home of the church in exile. But more than that, Cardinal Doria gave the Church his word that, with patient preparation, the time would surely come when the Holy See was recaptured, the invasion extinguished, and, God willing, all captives freed.

Despite his captivity, Clement received word of the desperate sentiments of large swaths of the faithful and of the revolt boiling within the Church. Nonetheless, he refused to turn his back on his position. "My function is now the highest function of this papacy," he reminded himself daily, "to keep open warfare from breaking out between the world's two largest faiths over possession of the Holy See."

As the weeks under the new order passed, Ali understood even more clearly that keeping Clement alive and able to act as titular, if truncated, head of the Roman Church was in his evolving interests. He began to allow Clement, under Hassan's watchful eye, to be in contact with certain bishops and others who appeared to remain loyal to his authority. At the same time, it was widely understood that many of those closest to Clement recognized that the pope was becoming increasingly enfeebled, both physically and mentally.

Soon Clement began making other statements, taking positions that further alienated him from the moderate and conservative elements in the Church. He began to say to all who would listen that the taking of the Vatican should be seen as part of God's purification of His Church. "Our love must not be for wealth or buildings or statues. God's kingdom is not of this world but in the hearts and actions of men. Nor does His religion depend on any place or piece of land." Although Clement continued to decry the deaths of so many at the start of the occupation, the destruction of the Church's material patrimony, he said, was different. To the amazement of the Church Universal, Clement argued that the losses recently suffered might well be a blessing—a "just" loss—and a sign of the coming renewal of the Faith through the rejection of the impediments of worldly and material goods.

To his most vocal opponents in the Church, Clement was now regarded as complicit in the greatest crime in two thousand years. "By his words and actions," Cardinal Doria declared publicly, "our Holy Father has done two things: He has left the church without an anchor, confused and scattered. Moreover, while doing serious harm to Holy Mother Church, he has also given to God's enemies a great gift—the gift of time—which they have needed to solidify their hold on the Holy City, the city of our faith, the city these infidels have desired to possess nearly above all others. New plans must be made, and made swiftly, before more time is lost— indeed, before the Church herself is lost."

The Reign of Chaos

For the next three months, chaos and bloodshed reigned as Ali's forces strove to expand the caliphate of the Twelfth Imam to encompass the entire west side of the Tiber from Lungotevere della Vittoria at its northern edge to Trastevere in the south. Forays were also made into the city's prosperous northern and eastern sections as the Twelvers sought to secure parts of the affluent areas around Piazza del Popolo and the Spanish Steps, but the Roman police were able to repel these attempts.

Having declared it to be the second headquarters of the Roman caliphate, a small band of the most fanatical Twelvers managed to capture and desecrate the Capuchin church of Santa Maria della Concezione, with its collection of four thousand skulls and bones of friars now long dead. The church was retaken within a day, but not before the Twelvers crushed every sainted skull and burned the interior to ashes. Very few of the invaders were able, or even willing, to escape the inferno they had set.

With the failure of the Twelvers' attempt to secure the "liberation," as they deemed it, of Rome, by far the greatest number of the marauders retreated to within the walls of the Vatican. There they were protected not only by the threat of the slaughter of the hostages, but above all by the command of Pope Clement. As the sovereign of the Holy See, he demanded that all parties refrain from any military activity and to allow him to do what he could do to bring about peace. In addition, the Iranians received permission from Ali—who remained, of course, the actual sovereign—to establish an embassy, staffed by a contingent of the Iranian Revolutionary Guard, within the territory of the caliphate. The Bahrainis, Russians, and Chinese were encouraged to, and soon did, set up consulates within the conquered territory. These consulates and their sister embassies in Rome proper were the essential conduits in the theft and sale of the treasures plundered from the Vatican.

After the initial shock of the invasion was over, small bands of Catholic ruffians made forays against a number of mosques and Islamic-controlled houses within Rome and its suburbs, even up to the impregnable walls of the Vatican. These raids were met with the favorite stratagem of the Twelvers: torture.

The threats of inflicting suffering and death on women and children coupled with Clement's fevered pleas for peace and forbearance kept most of the outside world from reinvading the Holy See, and the torture of any young man the Twelvers might capture helped to keep such raids to a minimum. The agonies of the captives were broadcast for the world to witness: cages containing two or three men in chains were filled with paper and oily rags and set ablaze, or captives were dismembered one limb at a time, conscious and screaming for the cameras.

Nor should it be overlooked that this century's scandals involving so many prelates and high officials left a feeling of indifference and worse to the fate of Catholicism in the minds of millions. Luckily for the Church, it often appeared that only Islam was disdained with greater ferocity.

Still, as Ali confided to Hassan, not only the capture of the Vatican but the Liberators' continued possession of it seemed easier than it should have been. "Proof for all the world to see," as Ali said, "that Allah has blessed our work."

Having served his purpose, the Holy Father was seen less and less—and heard not at all—in the various video feeds put out by the caliphate. Twice a week a "message of peace" came out over the pope's name, but they were obviously written by Hassan and his henchmen. Except for brief shots of the stooped and aging pontiff hobbling through the gardens at eventide, Clement had become the invisible pope, the pope of captive acquiescence.

The Holy Father quietly prayed each day for death. If he was found kneeling or praying aloud, he was beaten. He was confined to three windowless rooms—a bedchamber, a bathroom, and a small study. Apart from an Italian copy of the Koran, his study contained no books.

Unable to perform any parts of his sacred office, Clement was quickly losing the ability to see himself as pope. Nonetheless, both the invaders and Clement understood that while he lived, he remained the ace the invaders held. Indeed, Clement was even more valuable than hostage children. Like the sword of Damocles, which is only useful as it hangs and useless when it finally falls, Pope Clement served a purpose to his captors only as pope and only while alive.

Unwilling Wife

S ister Irene lay on a flat sleeping pad quietly praying for death as she tried to shut out the awful sounds of her "husband," Hussein, having relations with his other wife in the next room. This went on every night. The worst of it was listening to Lucia, a young Italian girl abducted from Rome's streets the first week of the raids, weep through it all.

Irene was too old, too physically undesirable to be Hussein's true wife, since he wanted not only his pleasures, but also to help populate the new caliphate with healthy young Muslims.

Each night, Irene endured the cries as if Lucia's agonies were her own. Every hour Irene regretted her decision to renounce her faith. If she hadn't, she, the other nuns, and all the children would be dead, but their suffering would have ended. Now the horrors continued.

Despite everything, Hussein was never uncivil to Irene. She was old enough to be his mother, his grandmother really, and he treated her with a measure of respect. She had, after all, converted, and therefore should no longer be seen as an outsider or infidel. Hussein had laid out the sleeping mat for her in a small room between the kitchen and the bedroom, and aside from expecting her to cook and clean, he bothered her not at all.

Irene had just one other task: to sweep and mop the papal chamber when Hussein "allowed" Hassan to "borrow" her twice a week.

The Message

C leaning bucket in hand, Irene marched silently, head bowed, darting sidelong looks at Masoud, the guard who always escorted her to the pope's rooms, not far from where she was kept with Hussein and Lucia on the grounds of the Vatican. Masoud gripped her arm, but never painfully tight, which confused Irene, given how badly he treated the pope during these sessions.

Masoud would always lead Irene through the door, then shove and lock the unresisting pope inside his bedroom, all the while roughly laughing and mocking the old man. Today, however, as Masoud was pushing the pope into his bedchamber, Clement resisted, then asked for the copy of the Koran lying on his chair.

"Please, I would like to read as this room is cleaned."

Masoud smiled rudely, enjoying the pope's submissive tone, and assented. Perhaps the old infidel would become a Muslim, and perhaps he, Masoud, would get the credit!

The pope grabbed the book and rushed into his bedroom.

He stood watching the door as he was locked inside. Though the pope knew Masoud to be a crude lout, there was no hint that he had ever tried to injure the cleaning lady.

Still, repellent as he was, Masoud's favorite act seemed to be urinating loudly in the toilet with the door open while making lewd comments. Given the brutality of this new regime, Clement understood that this was the smallest instance of harassment. Nonetheless, because it was so personal, he found it acutely degrading.

But he didn't have time to worry about that now. Clement opened the Koran and carefully tore a long, thin strip along one of the margins. Then, in the smallest print possible, he took a pencil he had managed to hide in his room, and wrote in Italian: "Find Via Angelo Emo 111. Whisper RCLaetare. They will take you to Orvieto. Tell Archbishop Toscano I resign." Then Clement stood by the locked door and waited, praying.

Finally, he heard the revolting noises that told him Masoud was facing the wall at the toilet. "This may be my only chance," Pope Clement whispered. "God have mercy on us all." He bent forward painfully and moved the tip of the slip of paper back and forth under his door.

From the other side Irene saw it, and with her broom swept the paper nonchalantly into her dustpan.

She threw the scrap of Koranic paper and all the dust that she had collected into a small bag. When she was finished cleaning she gathered her things, which Masoud took as the sign to let the pope out of his bedroom. "Hurry up old man," Masoud grumbled, shoving the pope forward. "You move slower and slower every day."

Clement and Irene locked eyes as he stumbled into the room. She nodded imperceptibly.

Escape

Irene's mind whirled as she lay on her sleeping mat that night. *Find Via Angelo Emo 111. Whisper RCLaetare. They will take you to Orvieto.* Pulling the paper from her bag while Masoud's back was turned, she had committed the pope's words to memory—then swallowed the paper! *Tell Archbishop Toscano I resign.*

Irene's heart pounded at the memory of her deed. Though she and Clement hadn't exchanged a word, Irene burned with the conviction that this was a mission of almost unimaginable importance. "I *must* get to Via Emo," she whispered to the ceiling.

Irene knew that the Via was close, just a few blocks from where she lay—but on the other side of the impenetrable west Vatican wall.

Deep into the night Irene remembered something. One day, not long after the invasion, on her way toward a house she was assigned to clean, she thought she'd seen a figure ahead walk beside the wall, then *disappear*—but when she reached the spot all she could see was a decayed portion of the wall completely covered with thick flowering quince and ivy. At the time, she could do no more than pause and stare, for fear of attracting unwanted attention. "I must have imagined it," she had told herself, but now that she really thought about it, the spot wasn't far from Via Angelo Emo—directly on the other side of that dark, dense wall.

There was no time to waste. Irene rose and dressed in black from burqa to walking shoes. She snuck out of the sleeping house, thanking God for Hussein's noisy snoring and a moonless sky. Irene hugged the shadows of buildings as she made her silent way toward the spot, managing to avoid the slowly passing headlights of the security vehicles patrolling the Vatican at night, praying with every step forward that she would remember correctly.

As she approached what she thought was the area she had seen the mysterious figure she began to run her hands along the wall. The quince bush thorns tore at her palms, but she bit her lip and continued to feel her way in the darkness.

Suddenly, the rumble of an engine broke the silence. Irene looked back and her heart leapt wildly. She could see the glare of headlights approaching.

And then she felt her hand slip through a crack in the wall and she nearly stumbled. Her painter's eye and memory had not failed her. She had found the spot!

With a deep breath, Irene lunged forward and pressed into the hidden hole in the wall. Thorns ripped at her clothes and what little flesh was exposed, but she managed to make it through.

Irene ran as fast as her old legs would move and hid in the shadows of a ruined building, struggling to catch her breath. She mouthed a prayer, certain she'd be discovered. But as she scanned the nearby apartment building and homes, all burned or destroyed, she was only met with silence.

"I can't believe there's a Christian left in all this rubble," she whispered as she stole forward along the darkened streets. Finally, there it was. *Via Angelo Emo 111.* With another quick prayer Irene stepped up to the door and knocked lightly.

After a long heart-stopping moment she heard quiet footsteps from inside.

"*Regina coeli laetare,*" she managed to utter, trembling.

Her words were greeted with absolute silence.

What was I thinking! Sneaking around like a thief in a Muslim neighborhood, speaking a Latin prayer to the Virgin Mary in the middle of the night to people I have no real reason to trust! What if the Holy Father was wrong? Irene fought back the panic. *I must have faith! I must have faith! I have faith.*

Finally a whispering voice answered. "*Resurrexit, Sicut dixit, Alleluia!*"

And the door opened.

Seen and Unseen

ussein was disconcerted to find Sister Irene's
sleeping mat empty the next morning. She had
returned from her cleaning chores the previous
day without mentioning anything, but perhaps she had
been called to do more scrubbing and sweeping today and
left quietly, so as not to disturb him, when one of Hassan's
guards came for her.

Hussein was aware that he was somewhat lax with Irene,
but she was only a woman—an old woman who reminded
him of his mother. That would hold water with no one,
however, not with Hassan and especially not with Ali. Hussein grew worried, for himself.

When Irene failed to return by late evening, Hussein
dragged himself, quaking from head to toe, to Ali's headquarters to relate what now must be reported. Enraged, Ali
had him beaten until he "remembered" what he did with
Irene or where she had gone. "No woman leaves her home
without her husband's knowledge!" Hussein was beaten
until he could no longer stand or see. But it was soon clear
that he knew nothing.

Masoud, however, was different. "Yes," he said proudly

when questioned. "The old lady came to clean the pope's rooms." Yes, "she was alone with me" the whole time. No, she and the pope never spoke—not once. "In fact, the old man was locked in his bedroom, studying the Koran!"

So Hassan went with Masoud to pay the pope a visit. "No, I did not see nor speak with the cleaning lady yesterday"— on this Masoud and the pope agreed. Hassan asked to see how much of the Koran Clement had studied. It didn't take long for Hassan to find the page with the torn margin, and, after a quick search of the pope's rooms, where the pencil was hidden.

The price for defacing the Koran was death, of course, and once he pieced together what must have taken place, Ali decreed that the pope should die, and die horribly. But not just yet.

The penalty for writing a note to the cleaning woman, however, was immediate: A surgeon was called who cut off both of Clement's thumbs and index fingers at the joint nearest the palms. The stumps were then cauterized with an iron.

For his seditious stupidity, Masoud was beheaded and his ugly head hung on a tree for the birds to eat. His unseeing eyes went first.

Where to Begin—and End

Farid and his wife Farrin were Iranian Christians living as Muslims in Rome. They were prosperous enough to have a summer villa in Orvieto, in Umbria, an hour by train north of Rome. Soon after they were wed, they began to have an interest in the Faith, and were baptized in a secret service in Orvieto going on twenty years earlier.

Since conversion meant death, they kept their Catholicism hidden from everyone in their families and from their Muslim neighbors. To all the world Farid and Farrin Khatami were staunch and faithful Muslims, and that's the way the Church wanted it to look. As converts working secretly within the Muslim community they were of great value. As martyrs for the Faith, less so.

Very few people knew Farid and Farrin's secret. The archbishop of Orvieto knew, the papal secretary of state (when he was alive) knew, and Pope Clement knew.

Moving quickly, they welcomed Sister Irene into their home and Farrin gave Irene the clothing of an Italian widow to wear. The black dress and black headscarf and shawl were not all that different from her nun's habit or her burqa.

Then they gave Irene a bowl of *ghormeh sabzi*—an herbed and lemony lamb stew—and many cups of sweetened tea to fortify her. They then invited her to rest comfortably until the first light of dawn, marveling privately at the old woman's stamina and faith.

After a hurried breakfast, Farrin handed Irene sixty Euros in bills and coin. They sat together in the back seat of the car as Farid drove to Termini railway station. On the way, the three prayed together before Farrin gave Irene these instructions: "Take the train going north, toward Milan. Get off at Orvieto, then take the funicular up to the city proper, and go to the Duomo. We will try to get word to the archbishop if we can. If we fail, inform him that Farid and Farrin sent you. Then, tell him all you know."

The hour-long train ride would give Irene some time to think about how to approach the archbishop. "But first," she told herself, "I have to think about where I hope the conversation *ends*, even before it begins."

Confession and Absolution

I rene reached the Duomo without incident. Having been directed to his residence, Irene told the guards that she had a message for Archbishop Toscano. Since she was plainly dressed as a poor widow, the head guard looked at Irene with disbelief and contempt. She knew she needed to speak with greater force: "I am Sister Irene, of the Augustinian Order of Sisters in the Convent of St. Paul in the Vatican. I have escaped from the invaders and bear all the wounds and scars of my flight. I have a message of the utmost importance to deliver to Archbishop Toscano. I will *not* move from this spot until he hears what I have to say."

Bewildered but moved by her conviction, the chief guard himself carried Irene's pronouncement to the archbishop, who studied his face before replying. "Have her patted down, then bring her to me. And stay with us."

"I bring a message of extreme importance from our Holy Father," Irene began without the ceremony of introductions, once she had been shown into the archbishop's office. "It's not a message I can share with anyone but you."

"Why should I trust you?" Toscano countered.

"Because our Holy Father directed me to two people

known only to you and to him," Irene answered, unfazed, "converts to the faith living in Rome, instructed and secretly baptized by you, who sent me here. Have your guard wait outside and I'll tell you their names. Once you know my fidelity to you and our Church, I'll tell you everything I know."

The archbishop rubbed his chin, then nodded to the guard to leave.

Once the door was shut, he invited Irene with a gesture of his hand to sit. The archbishop looked immeasurably weary. *Who doesn't these days?* Irene thought. *We priests and nuns are just men and women after all, living in times of turmoil and fear the Church has not seen since the Reformation and its bloody wars.*

"I was until two days ago housekeeper to our pope," Irene began. "He gave me a message to deliver to you. It said 'Find Via Angelo Emo 111. Whisper RCLaetare. They will take you to Orvieto. Tell Archbishop Toscano I resign.' There I found Farid and Farrin Khatami, the Christian couple who, at their own risk, helped me get here to you."

Toscano leaned forward and turned pale. *This is no ruse*, he thought. *This changes everything.*

He pushed a buzzer by his desk and ordered a large pot of tea and sandwiches. When the tray arrived, he told the guard to allow absolutely no one to disturb them.

With that, Irene's story poured forth. When she finally leaned back in her chair and fell silent, Toscano stood up and began to pace. "Tell me, how many children are they holding hostage? Are any prelates still living? Has the entire Vatican been despoiled?" Then came the most momentous question: "How much liberty does this message from Clement give us? We have refrained until now from doing anything at the pope's insistence. This message indicates a change of heart."

"Yes," Irene answered with firmness—though her answer reflected her own conclusions rather than any direct knowledge of the pope's thoughts. "Yes, I believe he has changed his mind. You see, all of the messages of peace now coming from the Vatican are written by the insurgents, not by him. About three weeks ago, when I was there cleaning his rooms, I witnessed an argument between our Holy Father and Ali, the leader of the invasion. 'You will read this as written,' Ali said. 'No,' Pope Clement replied with conviction. 'I can no longer say such things. All my words of peace get twisted and the situation becomes worse. With you, there is no peace.' Ali slapped him across the face! 'I have neither fear of you nor fear of death!' the pope shouted. His voice was so strong. He understands our situation is hopeless, and that it grows worse with every hour. He truly has no fear of death. I believe he awaits death with hope." Irene put her face in her hands and wept.

When she finally looked up, Irene asked for absolution for her apostasy from the Faith.

"It is granted," the archbishop said, making the sign of the cross, "without penance. Your penance was carried out long before this absolution."

Sister Irene had only one other request—to be rid of her widow's garb and once again wear the habit of her order.

Inquest

After being served a fortifying supper of vegetables and a Milanese risotto with saffron, cheese, and beef marrow, Irene was shown to a comfortable guest room in the archbishop's quarters. The tired sister took a warm bath—a hard-missed blessing!—and thought about what she must be prepared for next. With that, she uttered a few brief prayers and slept soundly.

After breakfast the next day, Archbishop Toscano's personal driver brought Sister Irene to Milan. She was to be grilled by Giovanni Doria, Cardinal Archbishop of Milan, around whom all those who had disparaged Pope Clement, all those who were eager to die for the restoration of their faith, and all those (religious or not) who wanted to destroy the invading Muslim forces and restore Italy to her former glory, had gathered.

It was deep in Cardinal Doria's nature to be skeptical. He understood well that the Devil—"the Prince of Lies"—was a genius at dissembling. So he peppered Irene with questions as if it were the Inquisition itself:

"Who was your mother superior and what has become of her?"

"Her name was Reverend Mother Margaret. Her name before she took on the habit was Felicia Cuneo. I heard the she is now in a cell, crippled and near death, having suffered horrible beatings for repeated insolence."

"Why is she insolent?"

"Because she knows, as do we all who are held against our will, that we are permitted to live as long as we are useful. If the liberation of the Vatican comes soon, we will be killed soon. If it never comes, if the world turns to other things, making us no longer useful, we will die then. But all of us now believe that a swift death would be a blessing."

Cardinal Doria paused to study the nun. "Exactly how did you get to Orvieto?"

Sister Irene related the story.

"And the Iranian couple who helped you escape, if I brought them here would they corroborate your improbable tale?"

"Yes, Your Eminence, though I fear they are no longer living since they never contacted Archbishop Toscano, as they said they would try to do."

"I see. And Pope Clement—now, as you say, the *former* Pope Clement—has made many shocking, foolish, and cowardly statements about the conquest of the Holy See. But the most foolish has been that we are forbidden to come to the aid of Rome because there would be bloodshed, especially the blood of innocents. Has he changed his mind about this? I command you to say only what you know."

Sister Irene hesitated, then, flooded with conviction, blurted out her answer. "Clement wishes for death because he knows that the longer he is safe the longer the invaders are safe and that they will grow daily in number and strength. The Holy Father no longer broadcasts his own prayers for peace and forbearance—these are written for him by the insurgents. Nor will he read them any longer. I believe he now well understands how mercilessly he has been used. I say all this based on what I have seen and lived. The lives of us captives secure the power of the infidels. Our prayers for peace have only strengthened their grip. We are the unwilling soldiers in their wicked campaign, and they have placed us at the front line!"

"How can you know that Clement believes as you do? You are nothing but a housekeeper."

"Truly, Your Eminence," Sister Irene said with supreme assurance, "I know *because* I am his housekeeper."

Cardinal Doria smiled. It was exactly the answer he wanted to hear.

Communion

The cardinal archbishop rang for *caffè* and pastry. "Thank you, Antonio," he said, when his butler arrived with the tray. "And stay away until I ring for you again."

He stirred his *caffè* and considered the closed door for a few moments. When he spoke again, Cardinal Doria's tone was less sharp, but more urgent. "There is much more I need to know. It is my intent to avenge all that these savages have taken from Holy Mother Church. But before I can finalize any plan to retake the Holy See I must understand *everything*.

"Tell me all you can about the leader of the insurgents, this Salvatore, who claimed to be the long-awaited Twelfth Imam of the Shi'a, but who is now dead. I've heard that he was an orphan, but I also heard an absurd story that he lived at your convent, then with the priests in the Vatican, and that his mother was actually a nun there."

"It's all true, Your Eminence. Salvatore was the son of Sister Maria Fidelis, conceived in rape by an Islamist. Of course, we never for a moment thought of aborting the child, and so we raised him first in the Vatican orphanage and then he lived with Father Adrian Faulkner and Father Balthasar Castellani—the chief Vatican scientist and the papal legate in charge of the Holy Shroud. These two holy and eminent priests were also Salvatore's teachers."

Sister Irene hesitated before continuing. "Salvatore was so smart, but then everyone began to notice that he was different, strange somehow. As he grew up he held himself apart from everything and everyone. And then he began leaving at night, and fell into the company of Islamists. He became defiant, rude to the fathers and my sister nuns. You see, Father Balthasar, well… he thought Salvatore was the actual and true reincarnation of Our Lord Jesus—"

The cardinal recoiled. "Don't cast into doubt all you've told me, Sister. This is blasphemy—or madness!"

"Well, Father Adrian certainly didn't believe Father Balthasar," Sister Irene responded. "It wasn't long before that terrible first day of the insurrection that Father Adrian called Reverend Mother Margaret and me to his office. He told us that he had reason to believe Salvatore was a fanatic, a monster on the verge of committing some horror—he knew that we all saw something terrible growing in Salvatore—and he was asking for our help in finding a way to shelter Sister Maria. He didn't want her to see what her son was capable of doing.

"So we devised a plan to have Sister Maria transferred to another convent so she could be nearer to her own mother, who was ailing. But then *everything* happened so quickly," Sister Irene wrung her hands at the memory. "Poor Maria was the last person Salvatore ordered killed—his own mother!—before Father Adrian finally stopped him."

"How?" Doria whispered.

Irene's voice broke. "He stabbed Salvatore to death with his own knife."

"I don't understand!" Cardinal Doria cried. "How could Father Balthasar believe such a monster was actually Our Lord Jesus Christ returned? And how do you even know that he did?"

"Father Adrian told Reverend Mother that Father Balthasar believed he had revivified Our Lord from the blood on the Holy Shroud. She told me this after they—Sister Maria, Father Adrian, Father Balthasar, and Salvatore—were all dead."

Conflict

The next day Cardinal Doria asked Sister Irene to re-tell her story, from beginning to end without leaving out a thing she'd already told him, to a private conference of his most trusted allies.

A heated discussion followed, to which Sister Irene was largely a silent and exhausted witness.

"I don't doubt that this Salvatore was the child of some Muslim rapist," said Monsignor Vidor Kardos, the cardinal's closest advisor. "These pigs are all over Europe—encouraged to roam and settle even by people of authority in the Church. Remember the foolish words of our previous pope: 'Better to accept all refugees than hide behind supposed security concerns.'"

"Who is so big a fool to think that this boy could be the reincarnation of some fanatical imam who lived ten centuries ago, let alone the Christ?" countered a young priest by the name of Alessandro. "Evil exists. He was an evil child who was becoming an evil man. Nothing more."

"I don't know what to think!" another prelate, Father Costa, argued. "The Church has never officially stated that the Shroud is real, but Father Balthasar was a scientist of great repute as well as a pious and respected priest. Perhaps he knew more than he had the chance to tell anyone."

"Silence, everyone," Cardinal Doria broke in, using the tone of one accustomed to being in charge. "If Father Balthasar truly did revive the person once covered by the Shroud, then that person was not Christ. And if he was directed to do so by a divine voice, that so-called divinity was not our God, our Father, but Satan, the Prince of Darkness. To believe otherwise is to believe that it was Allah who gave your deceived Father Balthasar the command!"

He turned to Sister Irene. "Tell us, what do the fanatics in Rome believe?"

Sister Irene's voice was small in the room, but all present hung on her every word. "They believe that Salvatore was the true and actual Twelfth Imam, the Hidden One come to restore the rule of Allah, here in Italy, then over all the earth. They believe, as Salvatore himself believed, that the blood on the Shroud was the Twelfth Imam's blood, and that, unwittingly, Father Balthasar did what Allah wanted him to do—to reintroduce the Hidden One back into the world. They even say that's why he was called Balthasar, after the last of the three magicians who followed the star, and who was called back to Earth by Allah to carry out the mystical work of revivifying the Imam. But Allah is all-powerful, they say, and he rightly discards those he uses when their time is over. I know all this because Hussein, the husband forced upon me by my captors, told me."

"And this fantasy was spread among the insurgents?"

"Yes, Your Eminence. And I believe that Father Adrian tried to warn others of what might be coming, but his words fell on deaf ears." The air grew tense at this, but Sister Irene pressed on. "And I can tell you that Father Adrian was *not* given to fantasy or invention." Her voice grew louder, more certain. "I knew him. I know that Clement said, when our troubles first began, that it was in part Adrian's violence that helped lead to so much blood. But I tell you, this is wrong. Father Adrian did what he had to do to avenge Sister Maria and to deprive the fanatics of their idol. He was a saintly priest who defended the Faith. *He deserves to be blessed, not questioned.* Father Balthasar was a good man, too. An infinitely good man. Kind and charitable and so very, very learned. If he committed a sin, he must have done it unwittingly, in the name of science. Please do not be harsh with his memory."

"His memory be damned!" the cardinal archbishop thundered. "Good, holy, and kind? I think we all would pray for the courage to do what Father Adrian did. But Balthasar? It's clear, from all that you have told us, that Balthasar was an arrogant man who heard voices that told him to commit an insanity. And in believing in the supremacy of his own all-too-human powers, Balthasar, not Adrian, became the agent of death for thousands—and if we don't stop the madness he started, perhaps millions."

The Battle Is Joined

Every September 29 the Church celebrates the feast of St. Michael the Archangel. On that day, every television the world over was focused on two people: Cardinal Archbishop Giovanni Doria and Sister Irene.

The cardinal archbishop was dressed in his most imposing scarlet robes. His eyes seemed more piercing, his voice more commanding, than ever. Sister Irene was in full habit, black and white, with only her lined, luminous, and brave face showing.

"Rumors abound that a hostage has escaped the tyranny of the infidels in the Vatican to bring news of our Holy Father and of those held captive," he began. "Those rumors are true. We have learned from that hostage, Sister Irene, that our Holy Father has resigned—abandoned—the papacy, and that the Chair of St. Peter is now vacant. We also know that many of the nuns and children taken hostage have been beaten, tortured, even killed." He turned and, nodding, stared at Sister Irene.

She spoke quietly and clearly, without hesitation. "What the cardinal has told you is true. The hostages pray for liberation or death. The beautiful women of Italy who have been captured and forced to become 'wives' and 'sex slaves' of the insurgents suffer every day at the cruel hands of their captors. I received word from the Holy Father himself that he has resigned his holy office. I tell you only what I know—the Church is now without a pope."

Doria resumed speaking "I have been in touch with many others in the hierarchy of the Church and we are all in accord: If Clement is rescued, he will be re-acclaimed as pope by the will of the whole Church. If not, a new conclave will be called and a new head of the Church selected—but not until Rome is set free and the cardinals can meet in the ruins of St. Peter's.

"To do this we must all act as one. I will continue to confer with those within the Church who agree with us—and I give you my word that this horror will soon be ended. But let me be clear: We will act with precision and resolve. When the appropriate time comes I will call upon all who wish to participate in the true liberation of God's Church to join with us to free the Holy See and Rome from these infidel marauders. All that is holy and just demands it, the Church prays for it, and God Himself wills it."

Just as it seemed that Doria had finished, he turned to look into the cameras with even greater intensity. "While we respect and take into account the words of Pope Clement counseling forbearance and nonviolence, this sacred day is the Feast of the Archangel Michael. If this day teaches us anything it is that even God our Father, when faced with fiendish evil, unleashed the heavenly hosts led by Saint Michael to destroy the Satanic mob and cast into hell the

Devil and all his followers always and forever. We can do no better than to follow the example of God Himself." Then he made the sign of the cross, saying, "As the great prayer of the Church instructs us, 'Saint Michael the Archangel, defend us in battle. Be our protection against the wickedness and snares of the Devil. May God rebuke him…and do thou,' Prince of the army of Heaven, aid us in casting into hell Satan and all his followers who today seek the ruin of souls and the destruction of God's Holy Church."

Even as these words were spoken a great and young army of the pious, the fanatical, the truly holy, and the adventurous unemployed had begun to assemble in assigned places over the northern half of Italy. They gathered in camps, on army bases, by schools and hospitals. And for every invader of the Holy See, for every Iranian Revolutionary Guardsman, for each Muslim defector from the Italian army, thirty, forty, fifty volunteers arrived, ready to march on the fallen Holy City.

From the safety of a screen Ali watched this transpire, as did virtually everyone else on Earth. He gave word to Hassan, who gave word to their many minions, that soon the battle would be joined, but "while the Christians are depending on an 'angel' to save them, we have Allah, Merciful and Compassionate, who will grant us an even greater victory than before!"

Once they were certain that the battle was imminent,

Ali and Hassan went to see the pope. They entered his rooms and found Clement kneeling at his bedside, immersed in prayer. He crossed himself with a disfigured hand and looked up at them. "Do what you have come to do."

Hassan held the Holy Father by the hair and pulled it back to expose his frail throat. Then Ali slit Clement's throat—nearly but not quite severing his head. They stripped the body and tied it to dangle naked by both ankles from the papal balcony.

Throughout the Vatican, all hostages were killed.

Call to Arms

Two days after Cardinal Doria and Sister Irene's first broadcast and its bloody aftermath, Monsignor Kardos received in his office a secret delegation of Muslims from Rome. They had come to reassure the cardinal that they were as horrified as he by the actions of these murderous Twelvers. More importantly, they had a plan they hoped the cardinal would approve.

The delegation was in earnest in trying to convince Cardinal Doria that they had in their congregations scores of liberal Muslims who were not enemies but friends of the Church, and that they spoke for many Muslims who were devoted to Imam Omar and who had quietly stood by him throughout the trials and insults he had suffered.

"We are prepared," Imam Aldouri, the leader of the delegation, declared, "to join with you in helping your forces regain the Holy See. We would like to offer you a plan." Aldouri then outlined how, with Doria's permission, he could create a small command group of two dozen or more faithful Muslim men to be the wedge that might enter the Vatican, with the Church's forces behind them.

Cardinal Doria looked wary. "But why should you come

to us like this?" he asked, staring directly into Aldouri's eyes. "And why should we believe that you and your Muslim clannishness is willing to join itself to the Universal Church so that you put yourselves at our service?"

Aldouri replied without rancor. "Forgive my forwardness. Please don't forget that the first people killed in this slaughter were of our 'clan': Imam Omar and his two young sons. We want to march in their honor, just as Imam Omar himself would have done. In truth, we need to avenge their deaths. By our silence we have done a great disservice to our brother Omar, and to Islam. Moreover, speaking Farsi as well as Arabic, we can present ourselves to the occupiers as armed reinforcements willing to fight by their side. If we succeed, I believe they will open the gates to us. As fellow Muslims with arms, we will not be turned away."

"Please, Your Excellency, if I may," Sister Irene suddenly interjected. "Omar and his two sons were slaughtered before Father Balthasar or Sister Maria or anyone else was killed. The insurgents carried their heads on sticks when they marched into the Vatican Gardens! They are, to all in the Church, three blessed Muslims, baptized in their blood. And those who would help us in their memory are righteous Muslims."

"*Blessed Omar? Righteous Muslims?*" Cardinal Doria stared at her with unalloyed disgust. Why Kardos had even allowed her into the meeting was inexplicable.

"I believe the good Sister is correct," Monsignor Kardos declared before a silent, frozen Doria. "Surely this is an offer we should seriously consider, Your Eminence." He turned to Aldouri. "My friend, please return to Rome and keep us apprised of the situation. Together, I believe we will all get justice for Omar and his sons, and recapture our most holy city. I am heartened, very heartened, by your generosity."

With that, the delegation departed. Cardinal Doria then, with steely thanks, excused Sister Irene as well.

"Are you mad?" Cardinal Doria asked Kardos once they were alone. "What is there to prevent these people from betraying us? And this Sister Irene, this Muslim apologist…"

"The woman has served her purpose, Your Eminence. But she is hardly the issue. The insurgents are the ones currently guarding the gates into Vatican City, and these so-called 'Righteous Muslims' are offering us a key. But more important, they will enter first. With our troops at their backs, I doubt if they can betray us."

While Doria and Kardos were debating, Sister Irene returned with an unsettled heart to the small room that had been assigned to her. Why did what should have been a positive, even joyful meeting with the Muslim delegation become so contentious?

As she often did when perplexed, Irene pulled out her sketchbook.

"Monsignor Kardos is terribly abrupt and sharp," she wrote, "but without his words of encouragement at the end, the cardinal would have pushed what I said aside and humiliated Imam Aldouri, who came offering only to help."

Irene studied her words, then began to sketch faces. First,

she tried to draw Monsignor Kardos, but no lines seemed to capture his nature. *Level-headed... Smart... Perhaps—but his true character seems hidden behind a mask.* She moved on to framing Cardinal Archbishop Doria's strong features. But unlike the portraits of great saints and martyrs she always painted, Doria's visage seemed less holy, colder, with eyes that bespoke not only intelligence but also some deep desire, some unfolding design.

Irene quickly ripped out the page of unfinished portraits, folded it, and slipped it into the back of her sketchbook.

Consumed

li ordered Amir and Hamid, two of his most trusted soldiers from the Iranian Revolutionary Guard who were experts in stealth, espionage, and assassination, to go to Turin and return with the Shroud.

He knew that this would hardly be an easy task. The Shroud was kept in a silver casket, housed in an iron box, all within a marble case. The case itself lay secured in the Chapel of the Holy Shroud, behind Turin's heavily guarded great cathedral.

Amir and Hamid's greatest challenge was moving about unobserved. When a custodian in the chapel noticed the same two visitors reappear over a number of days he reported it to his superior, who told the bishop of Turin, who got word to Cardinal Doria in Milan, just over an hour away.

Amir and Hamid were planning to start a fire in the main church to distract the authorities away from the chapel. They solicited four trustworthy local Islamists to start the blaze and then, when the police and firefighters arrived to save the cathedral from destruction, these men would shoot everyone in the church as well as anyone trying to enter, to make the distraction complete. During the turmoil, Amir, Hamid, and their accomplices would enter the Chapel of the Shroud, destroy the marble case, set the chapel ablaze, and steal the silver casket containing the Holy Shroud of Islam.

But even as these preparations were underway, Cardinal Doria was heading to Turin, where, upon his arrival, he directed the custodian to remove the Shroud from its case and place it in a cedar box kept under his control. Doria had four guards secretly stationed within the chapel.

Remembering the fires that the invaders had set right after the initial invasion and the burning of the Capuchin church, Doria said to the four, "Wait until the doors are breached, wait until the marble box is opened, and, if fires are started, let them burn. Then, *on my command*, fire on the invaders—and shoot to kill!"

Within minutes of the commotion set off in the main church, Hamid and Amir and their small band of ruffians entered the chapel. They broke the marble case, broke the lock on the iron box, and took the silver casket. They were setting fires behind them as they moved toward the door when Hamid opened the casket. "It's empty!" he shouted.

Hamid raced back to the altar, coughing on the smoke from the growing fires he and his men had set.

Cardinal Doria himself stepped from behind the altar. He held up the cedar box. "Is this what you seek?"

He placed the box on a wooden kneeler next to the flames.

Hamid lunged—and Doria gave the order to shoot.

Two guards grabbed the cardinal, pulling him through

haze and smoke, over the bodies of the invaders, and out to safety. Both chapel and cathedral were engulfed in flames. And the cedar box containing the Shroud was left in the path of the conflagration set by Ali's men.

Tumbling

The next day, the cardinal appeared again on television, this time alone. "The invaders are now expanding their terror far beyond Rome. Yesterday, they set fire to the Chapel of the Holy Shroud in Turin, destroying with their own hands this holiest of Christian relics. I was there. I tried to defend the Shroud, but it was ripped from my grasp. I did all I could to save it, but just as I fought to recover the sacred cloth, two heroic guards pulled me from the flames before I perished."

"Given this abominable sacrilege," he declared, "I believe the hour to act has come."

The band of Righteous Muslims had wasted no time in making secret contact with Ali, assuring him of their fealty to his cause and offering him two dozen armored vehicles, a range of explosives, and thousands of rounds for their AK-47s.

Their words of loyalty were quickly sealed with oaths, for Ali was well aware that the scores of Christian militias, having gathered under the command of Cardinal Doria and with the complete support of the regular Italian army, were camped on all the hills that surrounded Rome.

They were ready and eager to liberate the city.

Two days after the burning of the Chapel of the Holy Shroud, Imam Aldouri contacted Cardinal Doria. "Ali has sent word to our Muslim auxiliaries to join with the Army of the Twelfth Imam in the defense of the city," he whispered, his voice strained. *"The battle begins tonight!"*

Treachery

Having gathered, the Righteous initiated battle through the Porta Pertusa, on the southwestern side of the Vatican. Following the exact strategy they had formulated with Kardos and Doria, rather than join the forces of the Twelvers, the Righteous Muslim vanguard entered, then mowed down everyone before them in their path. Surprised by the treachery of Muslim against Muslim, Ali's men fell like hay before the reaper.

At Monsignor Kardos's insistence, and as a sign of their holiness and willingness to die for the Church and for Rome, all of Cardinal Doria's encamped soldiers wore a cross stitched on their chests and on their backs. Once inside the city, only those wearing a cross would be spared.

Soon after the opening of the great Porta, after the platoon of the Righteous had killed so many, these crusaders entered behind them, bringing more bloodshed than anyone could have imagined possible.

And, when dawn broke the next day, only the hoard of Doria's crusaders was left standing. Every Twelver lay dead.

And every one of the Righteous—brave men without crosses on their backs—also slain.

AFTERMATH

Amid the Ruins

T he next day Cardinal Archbishop Doria, his entourage, and over a hundred select prelates entered Vatican City and tied the papal flag to a broken column in St. Peter's Square. A contingent of Italian soldiers and Roman police collected the arms and drove or towed off all the vehicles.

Members of the Iranian Embassy and the other consulates—under immunity and unharmed in the fighting—were escorted out of the Vatican. The bodies of the dead were piled up in the campo, where Father Balthasar, Father Adrian, Sister Maria, and so many others had been killed, awaiting permitted members of the Roman Muslim community to reclaim and bury the corpses of the Muslim dead.

Pope Clement's naked body was found still hanging from the balcony of his apartment. His head—with black sunken eyes and gaping mouth—hung by a flap of skin at the back of his neck. Cardinal Doria had the body encased in a marble sarcophagus and set it in a flat area just off the Gardens. Covered with the finest linens and scores of vases of flowers, it would serve as a temporary altar until a proper burial could be arranged. Soon, it was the site of the first

Mass said in the Vatican since the invasion.

With outward signs of anguish and many tears, Cardinal Archbishop Giovanni Doria undertook the reconstruction of the Holy City. Restoration, wherever possible, was begun. New construction—paid for by the alms of Catholics worldwide—was planned. Most important, a new conclave was called. A new pope had to be elected quickly lest the body of Christ's Church be dismembered into regional or racial and ethnic factions.

On December 8, the Feast of the Immaculate Conception, the conclave was convened. The cardinals who came were housed in what remained of the buildings that survived the first invasion and the retaking. The election of the next pope was held in the open, on the broken foundations of the Basilica of St. Peter. It was a conclave held in view of all the world. They called it, appropriately, the Conclave amid the Ruins.

Sudden Certainties

S ister Irene worried that it would be a quick election, and she was right. On the first day, Giovanni Doria was elected pope by acclamation. He took the name of Innocent XIV.

Sister Irene had previously asked Cardinal Doria if she could attend the conclave with him and once again take up residence in the Convent of St. Paul, where she had lived for many decades and hoped now to live out her life.

He declined.

After Innocent's election, she wrote a letter asking not for any favors but for an official and private audience. The new pope referred the request to Monsignor Kardos, who knew how to respond.

"My dear Sister, although he cannot see you, if you will tell me the nature of this 'private' talk you wish to have with our Holy Father, perhaps you and I can see what can be done."

"I have many questions, but I don't believe you can answer them," Sister Irene replied, customarily forthright. She had so many—now that she'd had a chance to think about everything that happened since she met Giovanni

Doria—

Why didn't His Eminence keep the wooden box holding the Holy Shroud close to him, so that it would also be saved when he was pulled from the flames?

Didn't he know that sending the Righteous Muslims into battle without wearing the sign of the cross was consigning them to death?

Why was the conclave held in the open, contrary to all our traditions, and not in absolute secret, where those with concerns about our Holy Father's acts could have been spoken to and satisfied?

But with no way to reach the Holy Father directly, Sister Irene finally decided to put them in writing.

She handed the list to a stone-faced Kardos.

The Monsignor responded in kind almost immediately:

Even in raising such questions you betray your tendency toward rash judgment and unholy suspicion. Our Holy Father will not see you, nor will I. Your request for an audience is permanently denied. Moreover, and most importantly, our Holy Father hereby commits you to live out your days in the closed convent where you currently reside, under a rule of prayer and total silence. Any violation in any way of this regulation laid upon you by the highest authority will bring upon you full and automatic excommunication.

Upon reading this order, what were swirling suspicions on Irene's part became certainties. She thought long about the role she unwittingly played in the death of so many due to her gullible complicity in Innocent's elevation. She thought about how even the most well-meaning had been used to satisfy Doria's ambitions. And she thought tearfully about how the Shroud of Christ seemed purposefully consigned to the fires by Doria. Now cut off from the world by a private papal order, Irene understood there was little she could do to stop what had been released.

But *little* is not *nothing*.

Yes, she would obey the order commanding silence. But, as with Clement, even if she could not speak she would write. True, this cost Clement his life, but like Clement, she too recognized that she had reached the end of her days. Like Clement, like Sister Margaret, her Mother Superior, who was insolent toward her captors, even like Joan of Arc, whose strength and holiness ultimately led to her being proclaimed a heretic and burned to death, Irene set out to record what she suspected and what she knew.

The detailed note she penned was addressed to Angelo Bianchi, a young reporter at *La Stampa*, a liberal newspaper based in Turin, the editorial pages of which had long been skeptical of Doria when he was Milan's cardinal. She trusted Bianchi—who was struck by Irene's strength and steadiness when he had interviewed her twice in the preceding months. It was he who compared her, in print, to Saint Joan, which made the old nun blush and, no doubt, made Doria furious.

With the note sealed in an envelope, she managed to slip it unseen to one of the gruff delivery men who arrived a few times each week to bring vegetables to her new prison. If by ill-luck he failed to get the letter delivered to the paper, she was prepared. She had other copies and other stratagems at the ready.

Those without fear of death have little fear of much else.

Epilogue

A li understood that the arrival of the crusaders was imminent. On the night before the final battle began, he went privately to the Iranian Embassy, where he gave Ambassador Survan a package he said *must* be given to the Grand Ayatollah in Tehran if he and his men were killed or captured. When Ali and his followers were killed, the ambassador, under immunity, returned home to Iran. He presented the Grand Ayatollah with a gilt casket, pulled from the ruins of St. Peter's. It was lined in red velvet and contained a note penned by Ali: *This is the knife that killed the Hidden Mahdi. This is his blood.*

Made in the USA
Middletown, DE
21 May 2019